ONE THURSDAY MORNING

DIAMOND LAKE SERIES: BOOK 1

T.K. CHAPIN

Branch Publishing

Unless otherwise indicated, Scripture taken from the Holy Bible, NEW INTERNATIONAL VERSION®, NIV® Copyright © 1973, 1978, 1984, 2011 by Biblica, Inc.® Used by permission. All rights reserved worldwide.

To claim a FREE Christian Romance visit offer.tkchapin.com

Version: 12.10.2019

ISBN: 978-1535245104

ISBN-13: 1535245107

My Prayer Journal

Be sure to check out this lovely companion prayer book on Amazon.com. Order your copy today and start your journey toward a more rich and vibrant prayer life with the Lord.

View on Amazon

Dedicated to my loving wife.
For all the years she has put up with me
And many more to come.

CONTENTS

AUTHOR'S NOTE

Thank you for choosing to read **One Thursday Morning**. I wrote this book to help inspire women and men around the globe to see that God has a plan for their lives even when all hope seems to be lost. I've seen too many women be abused and stay with evil men because they think its love. There's a message of hope for every single person out there, and that is in the Lord Jesus Christ. It's only through a relationship with God that we can find true freedom.

And we know that in all things God works for the good of those who love him, who have been called according to his purpose.
Romans 8:28

If you or someone you know suffers from abuse please get help today. You can check out this website (click/tap here) to learn more about abuse.

PROLOGUE

o love and be loved—it was all I ever wanted. Nobody could ever convince me John was a bad man. He made me feel loved when I did not know what love was. I was his and he was mine. It was perfect . . . or at least, I thought it was.

I cannot pinpoint why everything changed in our lives, but it did—and for the worst. My protector, my savior, and my whole world came crashing down like a heavy spring downpour. The first time he struck me, I remember thinking it was just an accident. He had been drinking earlier in the day with his friends and came stumbling home late that night. The lights were low throughout the house because I had already gone to bed. I remember hearing the car pull up outside in the driveway. Leaping to my feet, I came rushing downstairs and through the kitchen to greet him. He swung, which I thought at the time was because I startled him, and the back side of his hand caught my cheek.

I should have known it wasn't an accident.

The second time was no accident at all, and I knew it. After a heavy night of drinking the night his father died, he came to the study where I was reading. Like a hunter looking for his prey, he came up behind me to the couch. Grabbing the back of my head and digging his fingers into my hair, he kinked my neck over the couch and asked me why I hadn't been faithful to him. I had no idea what he was talking about, so out of sheer fear, I began to cry. John took that as a sign of guilt and backhanded me across the face. It was hard enough to leave a bruise the following day. I stayed with him anyway. I'd put a little extra makeup on around my eyes or anywhere else when marks were left. I didn't stay because I was stupid, but because I loved him. I kept telling myself that our love could get us through this. The night of his father's death, I blamed his outburst on the loss of his father. It was too much for him to handle, and he was just letting out steam. I swore to love him through the good times and the bad. This was just one of the bad times.

Each time he'd hit me, I'd come up with a reason or excuse for the behavior. There was always a reason, at least in my mind, as to why John hit me. Then one time, after a really bad injury, I sought help from my mother before she passed away. The closest thing to a saint on earth, she dealt with my father's abuse for decades before he died. She was a devout Christian, but a warped idea of love plagued my mother her entire life. She told me, 'What therefore God hath joined together, let not man put asunder.' That one piece of advice she gave me months before passing made me suffer through a marriage with John for another five trying years.

Each day with John as a husband was a day full of prayer. I would pray for him not to drink, and sometimes, he didn't —those were the days I felt God had listened to my pleas. On the days he came home drunk and swinging, I felt alone, like God had left me to die by my husband's hands. Fear was a cornerstone of our relationship, in my eyes, and I hated it. As the years piled onto one another, I began to deal with two entirely different people when it came to John. There was the John who would give me everything I need in life and bring flowers home on the days he was sober, and then there was John, the drunk, who would bring insults and injury instead of flowers.

I knew something needed to desperately change in my life, but I didn't have the courage. Then one day, it all changed when two little pink lines told me to run and never look back.

CHAPTER 1

ingers glided against the skin of my arm as I lay on my side looking into John's big, gorgeous brown eyes. It was morning, so I knew he was sober, and for a moment, I thought maybe, just maybe I could tell him about the baby growing inside me. Flashes of a shared excitement between us blinked through my mind. He'd love having a baby around the house. *He really would.* Behind those eyes, I saw the man I fell in love with years ago down in Times Square in New York City. Those eyes were the same ones that brought me into a world of love and security I had never known before. Moments like that made it hard to hate him. Peering over at his hand that was tracing the side of my body, I saw the cut on his knuckles from where he had smashed the coffee table a few nights ago. My heart retracted the notion of telling him about the baby. I knew John would be dangerous for a child.

Chills shivered up my spine as his fingers traced from my arm to the curve of my back. *Could I be strong enough to live without him?* I wondered as the fears sank back down into me. Even if he was a bit mean, he had a way of charming me like no other man I had ever met in my life. He knew how to touch gently, look deeply and make love passionately. It was only when he drank that his demons came out.

"Want me to make you some breakfast?" I asked, slipping out of his touch and from the bed to my feet. His touches were enjoyable, but I wanted to get used to not having them. My mind often jumped back and forth between leaving, not leaving, and something vaguely in between. It was hard.

John smiled up at me from the bed with what made me feel like love in his eyes. I suddenly began to feel bad about the plan to leave, but I knew he couldn't be trusted with a child. *Keep it together.*

"Sure, babe. That'd be great." He brought his muscular arms from out of the covers and put them behind his head. My eyes traced his biceps and face. Wavy brown hair and a jawline that was defined made him breathtakingly gorgeous. Flashes of last night's passion bombarded my mind. He didn't drink, and that meant one thing—we made love. It started in the main living room just off the foyer. I was enjoying my evening cup of tea while the fireplace was lit when suddenly, John came home early. I was worried at first, but when he leaned over the couch and pulled back my blonde hair, he planted a tender kiss on my neck. I knew right in that moment that it was going to be a good night. Hoisting me up from the couch with those arms and pressing me against the wall near the fireplace, John's passion fell from his lips and onto the skin of my neck as I wrapped my arms around him.

The heat between John and me was undeniable, and it made the thoughts of leaving him that much harder. It was during those moments of pure passion that I could still see the bits of the John I once knew—the part of John that didn't scare me and had the ability to make me feel safe, and the part of him that I never wanted to lose.

"All right," I replied with a smile as I broke away from my

thoughts. Leaving down the hallway, I pushed last night out of my mind and focused on the tasks ahead.

Retrieving the carton of eggs from the fridge in the kitchen, I shut the door and was startled when John was standing on the other side. Jumping, I let out a squeak. "John!"

He tilted his head and slipped closer to me. With nothing on but his boxer briefs, he backed me against the counter and let his hand slide the corner of my shirt up my side. He leaned closer to me. I felt the warmth of his breath on my skin as my back arched against the counter top. He licked his lips instinctively to moisten them and then gently let them find their way to my neck. "Serenah . . ." he said in a smooth, seductive voice.

"Let me make you breakfast," I said as I set the carton down on the counter behind me and turned my neck into him to stop the kissing.

His eyebrows rose as he pulled away from my body and released. His eyes met mine. There it was—the change. "*Fine.*"

"What?" I replied as I turned and pulled down a frying pan that hung above the island counter.

"Nothing. Nothing. I have to go shower." He left down the hallway without a word, but I could sense tension in his tone.

Waiting for the shower to turn on after he walked into the bathroom and slammed the door, I began to cook his eggs. When a few minutes had passed and I hadn't heard the water start running, I lifted my eyes and looked down the hallway.

There he was.

John stood at the end of hallway, watching me. Standing in the shifting shadows of the long hallway, he was more than creepy. He often did that type of thing, but it came later in the marriage, not early on and only at home. I never knew how long he was standing there before I caught him, but he'd always break away after being seen. He had a sick obsession of studying me like I was some sort of weird science project of his.

I didn't like it all, but it was part of who he had become. *Not much longer,* I reminded myself.

I smiled down the hallway at him, and he returned to the bathroom to finally take his shower. As I heard the water come on, I finished the eggs and set the frying pan off the burner. Dumping the eggs onto a plate, I set the pan in the sink and headed to the piano in the main living room. Pulling the bench out from under the piano, I got down on my hands and knees and lifted the flap of carpet that was squared off. Removing the plank of wood that concealed my secret area, I retrieved the metal box and opened it.

Freedom.

Ever since he hit me that second time, a part of me knew we'd never have the forever marriage I pictured, so in case I was right, I began saving money here and there. I had been able to save just over ten thousand dollars. A fibbed high-priced manicure here, a few non-existent shopping trips with friends there. It added up, and John had not the foggiest clue, since he was too much of an egomaniac to pay attention to anything that didn't directly affect him. Sure, it was his money, but money wasn't really 'a thing' to us. We were beyond that. My eyes looked at the money in the stash and then over at the bus ticket to Seattle dated for four days from now. I could hardly believe it. I was really going to finally leave him after all this time. Amongst the cash and bus ticket, there was a cheap pay-as-you go cellphone and a fake ID. I had to check that box at least once a day ever since I found out about my pregnancy to make sure he hadn't found it. I was scared to leave, but whenever I felt that way, I rubbed my pregnant thirteen-week belly, and I knew I had to do what was best for *us.* Putting the box back into the floor, I was straightening out the carpet when suddenly, John's breathing settled into my ears behind me.

"What are you doing?" he asked, towel draped around his waist behind me. *I should have just waited until he left for work . . . What were you thinking, Serenah?* My thoughts scolded me.

Slamming my head into the bottom of the piano, I grabbed my head and backed out as I let out a groan. "There was a crumb on the carpet."

"What? Underneath the piano?" he asked.

Anxiety rose within me like a storm at sea. Using the bench for leverage, I placed a hand on it and began to get up. When I didn't respond to his question quick enough, he shoved my arm that was propped on the piano bench, causing me to smash my eye into the corner of the bench. Pain radiated through my skull as I cupped my eye and began to cry.

"Oh, please. That barely hurt you."

I didn't respond. Falling the rest of the way to the floor, I cupped my eye and hoped he'd just leave. Letting out a heavy sigh, he got down, still in his towel, and put his hand on my shoulder. "I'm sorry, honey."

Jerking my shoulder away from him, I replied, "Go away!"

He stood up and left.

John hurt me sober? Rising to my feet, I headed into the half-bathroom across the living room and looked into the mirror. My eye was blood red—he had popped a blood vessel. Tears welled in my eyes as my eyebrows furrowed in disgust.

Four days wasn't soon enough to leave—I was leaving today.

CHAPTER 2

*L*eaving my husband wasn't going to be easy, especially with his connections and the amount of money he could throw toward tracking me down wherever I went. John thought of me as a stupid dependent woman who relied heavily on him—I wasn't. I was smart and did a great deal of thinking about my plan to leave. I thought of who he would call, what he would do, and just what extremes he'd be willing to go to in order to stop me. I knew I was truly John's world—his everything. Without me here to fold his laundry and be his personal punching bag, he'd be a hopeless wreck.

In order to make it out alive, I would need to move quickly and not leave a trail of clues for him and his police chief's buddies to find. Vanishing wasn't exactly easy, but it could be done.

A few weeks ago, I traveled to Burlington in Vermont, which was over a three-hour drive from Albany, New York, where I lived. That trip was just to get a fake ID. My friend, Debbie Wadsworth, was kind enough to let me not only use her for an alibi for John, but also to let me know about our

11

old high school classmate, Milton Dewy, who was involved with a bunch of shady stuff in Burlington. She had heard he got busted a couple of different times for distributing fake IDs through another friend. She said he was selling them to students on high school campuses and that there was a good chance he was still making them. I made a day trip over to Burlington and got the ID after a painful hunt across eight different campuses. That day wasn't easy, but I felt it was vital if I was going to remain invisible once I left.

As the front door shut that morning when John left for work, I waited patiently at the kitchen table with my cup of coffee in hand. John had a bad habit of always leaving something behind in the mornings on his way out to work. The front door opened moments later. He said through the foyer, "Kind of need car keys to go. Eh?"

I forced that fake smile one last time onto my face. I stood up and retrieved his keys from the counter and headed to the foyer. Coming to him, my heart pounded and sweat began to bead on my forehead. *You can do this.* Leaning in, I let my lips catch his bottom lip. Even the most evil man I had grown to know had qualities I couldn't help but know I'd miss. Drinking in his distinct smell, I let my lips glide down his neck and to his collar.

"What are you doing?" he asked inquisitively as he reluctantly pulled back. "Why are you torturing me when I have to leave for work?"

"I'm just going to *miss* you." My double meaning hid behind my eyes, but it was fully seen and felt within my own heart. Soon, I'd be on a new path in life, and the painful memories that were stored away in the walls of this house would be nothing but a forgotten nightmare.

He smiled and tipped his chin with an air of arrogance. "Tonight, I want to take you out to the city. It'll be fun. We'll eat, dance, and get a hotel."

Though I hated the man, I had pleasant memories mingled in with painful ones. "Yeah, let's do that," I replied, smiling as I thought about all the memories of New York City I had with him. There was one night we had in the city that I'll never forget. It was the closest thing to magic I had ever found in real life. Our fingers intertwined with one another as we walked down Times Square, headed to catch a movie after a late dinner. The lights, the people, the energy. Everything felt so alive and vibrant. When one of my feet almost landed in a puddle, John caught me up in his arms and carried me over it just to avoid it. It was sweet. The best part was that he ended up stepping into a different puddle nearby. For some reason, it was funny and we laughed. Falling into his chest, I remembered feeling as alive like the city was that night. I'll never forget how happy I was. My cheeks burned that night just as I'd grown to expect, but not because John hit me, but because he'd made me smile.

When John finally left the house that morning and the door latched shut, I could almost hear the ending of this chapter of my life. The lies, the pain, the hurt . . . he wasn't going to be able to hurt me anymore where I was going. And while I loved the idea of him never again being able to hurt me like he had before, a part of me felt scared.

I went into the bedroom and began packing the gym bag. I began to think about how much easier it would have been if I didn't still love him, if somehow, I could have cut that part out of my heart. Glancing over, I saw one of his empty bottles of whiskey sitting on his nightstand—it helped dull the pain of packing. Stopping a few minutes into packing, I pressed a hand against my forehead. *He's going to be a wreck.* The problem was that I did love him, and I couldn't help but worry about him being alone with nothing but the bottle. My eyes fell to a blood stain on the carpet in our bedroom.

Seeing my own blood on the carpet helped push away the worry for John and motivated me to finish packing.

After the bedroom, I headed into the living room with the gym bag on my shoulder and retrieved the metal box from the floor beneath the piano. Shoving the money from my stash into the bag, my hands couldn't help but tremble. *This is it. I'm really going to leave him.* Turning off my cellphone, I tossed it, along with my purse, into the metal box. With the remainders of my old life in a ten inch by ten inch metal box, I latched it shut and placed it back into the floor. I fixed the carpet to make it look perfect, then I stood up and walked out the front door.

CHAPTER 3

One year later...

Balancing five plates of food between my two arms, I wove in a zig-zag pattern through Dixie's Diner, dodging other servers and tables along the way. Arriving to the family of five that sat in the corner booth of the restaurant, I smiled. A pencil behind my ear, an apron on my waist, and just enough energy to get through the day was my new life in Newport, Washington. It wasn't a glamorous life, but it was *mine* and it was away from John. *Love*, for the time being, only existed in the pages of the novels I read, the movies I watched, and in the couples or families that would come into the diner. I was okay with that fact. I needed the time over the last twelve months to allow my heart to heal, my life to rebuild, and my outlook to change.

Over the course of twelve months, I realized just how delusional I had been when I was with John. My idea of love back then was warped. I learned this through many hours of therapy down at 'A New Me in Christ' Christian Counseling Center in the neighboring city of Spokane. My idea of love had relied heavily on however John was feeling that particular day. If John came home and made love to me and didn't beat me, I felt loved. Counseling was a tough decision to follow through with, but it came after miscarrying my baby girl, whom I named Hope, at fifteen weeks pregnant. Her loss was devastating to me. After losing her, I became depressed and felt hopeless, without a reason to live. Depression seeped into my existence and crushed my spirit, and then one night, I decided to end my life with a bottle of sleeping pills. Before I did, though, I stumbled upon a Gideon Bible inside a nightstand in a cheap hotel in downtown Spokane. I started reading right where I opened— Psalms. And when I came to Psalms 46, my heart clung to the words like thirst to water in a dry place.

God is our refuge and strength, an ever-present help in trouble.
Therefore we will not fear, though the earth give way and the
mountains fall into the heart of the sea.
Psalm 46:1-2

IT WAS THE SAME VERSE THAT MY MOTHER READ AT HER OWN mother's funeral. Though I had abandoned my faith in my teenage years, I returned to Jesus that night. Asking Him to rule over my life on June 1, 2014 at 1:12AM, in a dimly lit hotel room with the sound of sirens in the background, I allowed God to be God again in my life.

Placing each plate of food in front of their respective owners at the table, I wiped my palms against my apron and asked, "Anything else?"

"No. I think we're good for now," the father said with a smile. *How come I can't find a guy like that?* Being in my late twenties, I was starting to notice a trend in a world outside of marriage. All the good guys were married, and anybody who wasn't . . . usually wasn't for a reason.

"Enjoy. I'll be back in a bit to check on you," I replied and left the table. The front door chimed, and I saw a couple that were regulars walk in—Sue and Frank. I held my breath a little as I watched them walk into my section minutes before I was scheduled to leave. My love for them ran deep, but my legs were exhausted. Seeing the couple sit down at a booth in my section, I scraped the bottom of my barrel of energy and pushed a smile out. Taking my pencil from behind my ear and the order pad from my apron, I walked over to them.

"Who let you two in here?" I asked jokingly.

They both laughed, and Frank asked, "How have you been holding up, Amy?" He was an older man who always wore an oil-stained, ragged hat and was missing a few of his teeth. He was, by far, one of the kindest people that I had met in Newport, always curious about my well-being and worried about me living out at the end of Piker's Drive, a gravel road just on the outskirts of town.

"Good," I replied as I tilted my head and flashed my smile to Sue. "Milo is good too. He's kind of an odd cat, but it's nice to have someone around."

Sue smiled back at me and then proceeded to say, "You should really get out to some of the community events more. Lots of the women around town go to them, and maybe you'll even meet a guy. You never know."

I kept my smile, even though my thoughts were anything but happy. "Thank you. We'll see. The usual for you two?"

"That'd be great," Frank said.

Jotting down their usual meatloaf and potatoes meal for the both of them, I turned and left the table. On the way back, I saw Miley at a table apologizing for a mix-up of some kind of order, and I laughed a little inside. *Gotta love when that happens.* Diego was on the line behind the server window and saw me attach the order slip to a clip above.

"Good evening. How's the battlefield?" he asked as he slid a hamburger patty onto a bun. Diego was a kind older man with a little mustache who worked hard to provide for his four children and wife at home. Dixie's Diner wasn't the only place he worked. He put quite a few hours in down at Lucky's Automotive too.

"It's busy tonight," I replied as I glanced over my shoulder at the packed out diner. "Guess that's all due to your mouth watering food."

He smiled and looked up at me for a moment. "I told you already, Amy. You can *have* the car. There's no reason to butter me up with compliments."

"C'mon. Just take the five hundred, Diego. I don't want it for free. I know you have mouths to feed."

He laughed. "You just can't let someone do something nice for you. Can you?" It was true. I couldn't. I felt an overwhelming desire to work for anything and everything that came my way after leaving John. I didn't want handouts. After a moment of quiet, he said, *"Fine.* I'll take the money. But you come to me for repairs if you need it."

"Amy," the manager, Wendy, said from behind me. Whirling around, I gripped the counter behind me and squeezed. She wasn't the most pleasant woman to work for, and intimidating didn't begin to describe her. A giant at a staggering six feet nine inches tall, she towered over anyone and everything around her. Once, making a joke about her relation to the fast food *Wendy's* girl had landed me with hours cut for the next month. She's all-around mean, but word on the street was she had good reason. Her husband of twenty years left her for his secretary—so cliché.

"Yes?" I asked.

"Number fourteen needs refills. Their cups are empty." Her tone was direct and flat. It was always that way.

Nodding, I peered through the crowded restaurant at table fourteen. Seeing the empty glass of a little boy sitting near the edge of the table, I flashed Wendy a polite smile and said, "Thanks."

DIEGO GAVE ME AND MY TEN-SPEED A LIFT TO MY HOUSE TO drop off the bike and to get the cash for him. I left the bike against the side of my house and got the money from inside. Getting back into his truck, we drove over to his house. As we pulled up in the driveway, the front porch light was on. Seeing the fenced yard, the sprinkler running, and a few stray toys littering the yard warmed my heart, even though it stung a little. *In your time, God. You know that in my heart, I want this someday.* We got out of his truck and headed up the driveway to the garage that sat in the back and connected to the alley. Going through the gate, we came around to the garage, and we both pulled up and pushed the garage door open.

Diego smiled as the dust settled and the 1971 lime green Ford Pinto came into view. "Not a pretty car, but it works," he said with a shrug.

Smiling, I nodded. "She's perfect."

"*She?*" Diego asked as I walked in and smoothed my hand across the dust-covered hood.

"Oh, yeah." Glancing in through the driver's side window, I continued, "This has too nice of an interior to not be a female."

He laughed and leaned to see past the garage toward his house. "It was my wife's car, but she doesn't use it anymore. She has one of those fancy SUVs nowadays. Hey, Amy," he said. Turning to him, I rose an eyebrow. "Here." He tossed the keys over. "Get in and get it out of here. I have to get inside to the wife and dinner."

I caught the keys and went over to Diego and gave him a hug. He was a great friend whom I viewed more like a father figure than a line cook at Dixie's Diner. He didn't have a lot of time in life, but he always took time to at least say 'hi' whenever he saw me. The first few months at the diner, when I was unsure of how to do my job, he helped. If I was falling behind, he'd run my food. If I didn't hear an order come up, he'd repeat himself. Always helpful. "Thank you."

"You're welcome, Amy. Run along now."

Hurrying back over to the car, I climbed inside. Dust thickened the air, but it did little to distract the smile that I found not only on my face, but in my heart. To have people who genuinely cared wasn't something I hoped to find when I left John. I never thought about that aspect in my new life, but I was glad I found it.

By the time I got back to my little house at the end of Piker's Drive, a summer rain had started in. Getting out of my car, I covered the top of my head the best that I could with my hands and hurried across the gravel up my porch. Unlocking the door and going inside, I was dismayed at the sight of water dripping from the ceiling. Shouting, I dropped the car keys on the entryway table, scaring Milo out of his nap and off the couch. I darted into the kitchen and grabbed a pot. As I positioned the pot under the drip, I realized how ironic it was that I'd forced Diego to take my money only a little while ago, and now, I had no money and a leaking roof. Laughing, I sat back onto the floor to pet Milo as I thought about the agreement I had with the landlord to fix any repairs myself to save fifty bucks a month in rent.

CHAPTER 4

On my break the next morning at Dixie's, I sat down in a booth and began calling around town to various roof contractors to see what the repair costs were for a leaky roof. There were no solid estimates on price for the repair since I wasn't sure how bad the leak was, but I was quoted six to nine hundred as an average based on the information I provided. Getting off the phone with a jerk from Spokane who said he'd be booked out until August—two months from now—I hung up, slamming my phone down in a stint of frustration. "Ugh! Why can't it just be simple?"

Emma Montgomery—the co-owner of Dixie's Diner—was nearby without my knowing and said, "Just gotta have a little faith."

Red with embarrassment, I looked over the booth at her. "Hey, Emma." She was an older woman, in her late seventies, but full of life. Though Emma didn't work at Dixie's, she would stop in on occasion to check on the operations of the place. There was more than one occasion that I sat with her and discussed all the taboo subjects of the work place. Things like God, politics and death were at the top of the list and a blast to speak about with her. She was my closest friend in Newport, and I cherished our relationship. My protective walls came down with Emma after hearing her testimony of meeting Jesus right after the loss of her own child years ago. We had a connection, something in common, and almost instantly became close friends. Emma was the first to know my real name because of working at Dixie's and the need to collect taxes with my social. She helped me set up a P.O. Box in Seattle to help deter John. She knew everything about me and promised not to tell a soul. I trusted her with ease.

Grasping the back of the booth, she worked her way into the seat across from me. Bringing her hands together on the table, she leaned in and smiled. "Joe's a good one. He charges reasonable rates if you haven't looked him up yet."

I nodded. "I called him, but he still wanted $550 even if it was simple." Running my fingers through my hair, I shook my head and met her eyes. "I shouldn't complain. I'm blessed. There's just no way I can pay for something like this up front, and most places won't accept payments."

Emma reached a hand out and grabbed my hand that was on the table. Giving it a squeeze, she said, "We all hit rough patches in life, kid. It happens. Would you work for the repair money at my inn? I know you won't just take the money."

"You're right, I won't. The B and B on the lake?"

"Yeah. *Inn at the Lake.* My daughter, Jody, and her husband, Wayne, need an extra hand around the—"

"Yes!" I replied, interrupting her before she could finish. Though I hadn't been to the lake often, I did make a few trips there over the course of the year since I had been in Newport. It was on a gorgeous lake, and I needed the money. "That would be great. I'm sure I'd love it."

"Have a strong back?" Emma asked with a raised brow.

"I don't know," I replied, wiggling in my seat as I adjusted my back to straighten it. "I think so?"

"Lots of landscaping work needs done around there." Emma reached for my pen next to the order pad on the table. Taking a slip of paper from the pad, she wrote down the inn's address and directions from the diner. "Head over there after your shift, and I'll let Jody know you're coming."

Smiling as I took the slip of paper, I said, "Thank you."

PULLING INTO THE DRIVEWAY, MY EYES WIDENED AT THE mansion-like Bed and Breakfast. The still waters of Diamond Lake painted a lovely backdrop for a breathtaking view. Parking beside a double garage, I got out of my Pinto without taking my eyes off the lake. The double oak doors opened down a few brick steps, and a little white-haired dog came running out as a woman stepped out of the doorway. She walked up the steps and met me in the driveway.

"I'm Jody Davis, and welcome to the *Inn at the Lake*. Do you have a reservation?" Her eyelashes fluttered and her hands came together at her waist. She was middle-aged, had short hair, and carried a constant smile.

"Emma sent me. I'm Amy," I replied.

A perplexed gaze indicated she never received a phone call. "My mother did? How does she know you?"

"The diner," I replied. "I serve there. She said you were looking for some help around here." My eyes surveyed the grass and pathways that led between the garage and the house and then the one that led around the side of the bed and breakfast and toward the water.

"Head around back and down to the shed by the water. You can find everything you need in there and start pulling weeds from the flower beds that line the path down to the lake. If you can handle it for two solid hours today, you can come back tomorrow."

"Okay," I replied. Before I could get another word in, she turned and went over to her puppy and picked it up before returning back inside. With no discussion of money, I felt a little uncomfortable getting started, but I knew Emma was involved and trusted her, so I pushed my worry aside. The cement path along the side of the house led me down a slight incline before veering over to a walking path that wove between flower beds down to an open grassy area where the shed and a dock sat. Once in the shed, I found a pair of gloves, a hand rake and a yard waste container.

Journeying over to the first flower bed I'd be working that day, I looked up to the balconies that hung off the bed and breakfast and took in the view of the overwhelming size of the house. It was bigger than any house I had seen since my arrival and even competed with the mansion John and I lived in back in Albany. Being on the lake, I couldn't even fathom what a house that size would cost. Though the decks weren't painted and the flower beds were full of weeds, it didn't take away the majestic and larger than life feeling that the whole place gave off. A man in his mid- to late-twenties stepped out onto the upper balcony and was looking out to the lake with his arms resting on the railing. He had a thick head of brown hair and a physique that was drool-worthy. The stubble along his jaw line only enhanced his rugged appearance, and he looked to be in deep thought as his eyes scanned the lake. Mid-drool, I realized I knew him from somewhere. *Who is that?* He pulled out a pocket watch and looked at it with a grimace. His piercing green eyes caught me staring, and he immediately shoved the pocket watch back into his pocket and left the balcony.

Starting in on the weeds that littered the flower bed, I blushed as I continued to attempt to place him. *He caught me staring like a weirdo. How embarrassing . . . but where do I know him from? And how on earth would I forget a gorgeous face like that?* It tortured me the entire two hours I worked. By the time I stood up from the flower bed, I still hadn't placed him, but I did feel pain radiating through my lower back. *How did my mom garden all those years while I was growing up?* Returning the gardening equipment to the shed with a wobble in my step, I grunted and groaned. Rubbing out the soreness the best I could, I made my way back up the path and around the house to the front doors where I first saw Jody. Straightening my posture the best I could, I gave a couple of good knocks on the door.

Jody answered and looked at my forehead, causing me to touch it. "You have a smudge of dirt on your face. Leave it. Come inside and let me get you a wash cloth from the kitchen." Pulling my hand, she brought me inside without waiting for me to answer. As she led me through a large foyer and around a corner toward the kitchen, she continued to talk. "The pay will be $100 a week and two hours a day. I spoke with my mother an hour ago, and she said you were trying to pay for a roof, so I'm willing to front you the money, and you can just work it off."

"I don't know about doing that . . ." I replied as we came into the kitchen.

Jody stopped and turned, placing a hand on the kitchen's island counter. Her eyebrows raised, and she said, "Amy. I understand you want to work for the money you get, but don't be dumb. Let me pay you in advance so your roof doesn't get more damage. I once had a roof that leaked, and we had to wait to repair it. Luck would have it that the place we were living at the time had the biggest storm in forty years that week of waiting, and I paid for it big time. So, please." Jody paused and smiled big as she let out a laugh before she continued, "just take it." She opened a drawer that was attached to the island and pulled out a checkbook. Writing out a check for six hundred, she ripped it out and handed it to me.

"Okay," I replied as I took it from her. Jody was a bit aggressive, but she was good-natured and had a sweet way about her.

She put the checkbook back in the drawer and went over to the sink. Grabbing a dampened washcloth, she held it out for me. I folded the check and slipped it into my back pocket before taking the rag to wipe the dirt off my forehead. *Emma must have told her to do that.* A smile crept up from the corner of my lips as I turned and looked across the kitchen and into the large, open dining room. What a perfect view of the lake through a pair of French doors. I said, "I love this property."

"It's beautiful. You can see the lake from every room in the inn. We are blessed to have it."

Handing her the rag, I said, "Thank you for the check and the washcloth. I appreciate you guys having me come out and help."

"We'll use you around here." She smiled and took the rag over to the sink and draped it across the faucet. She walked me to the front doors to leave.

On the way home, I called Joe, the contractor that Emma told me about, and set up a time for him to come by Thursday morning for an estimate on the roof. Things were going to work out, all thanks to the kind hearts of Emma and her daughter. It warmed my soul to have people in my life who not only cared, but were willing to help in any way they could.

CHAPTER 5

On the following Thursday, I waited for Joe to show up at the scheduled time of eight o'clock. By ten minutes past the hour, I was becoming a bit impatient as I had to be at work by nine. Leaning on the railing on my porch, I tried to see through the thicket of trees that lined the property, but it hid the gravel road from view. This was despite the fact that I knew I'd hear him before I saw him. Pressing up on my tiptoes, the weight of my body was too much for the railing, and it shifted forward. Jumping back, I crossed my arms. *This place is going to fall apart!*

The sound of wheels kicking up gravel a moment later brought relief over me. My tense shoulders relaxed and I dropped my arms as I walked over to the porch steps. He was finally here. Only fifteen minutes late. He pulled his truck up beside my Pinto in the driveway, got out, tipped me a nod, and then moseyed to the back of his truck. His worn-out jeans and tank top didn't scream professional, and his lack of urgency didn't do him any favors either. He bobbed his head as he dropped the tailgate. I had enough and headed out to his truck.

"You're late," I said curtly as I walked to his truck.

He raised an eyebrow and said over his shoulder to me, "Sorry 'bout that, Miss," as he reached into his truck with one of his muscular arms draped across the bed. The top of his shoulder flexed as he slid out a ladder from the bed of the truck. *It's been too long since I've felt the touch of a man if this guy can catch my interest.* He began walking over to the house. I followed him like a game of cat and mouse.

"Do you always show up late to jobs?" I pressed him.

"No." Arriving over beside the porch, he positioned the ladder against the ledge of the roof and squinted as he peered up. There was little interest on his face about his lack of punctuality. It didn't seem to matter to him in any way whatsoever.

"Do you even want to see where the leak is coming from inside?" I asked, slightly confused why he wasn't talking much.

He looked at me with piercing brown eyes and broke into a smile. "Well, yes. That'd be helpful."

Leading him inside, I held the screen door open for him as he walked through first. The whiff of his cologne caught my nose, and I felt a part of my stomach jump. *Stop it, Sere-nah! He's a paid professional . . . well, he's getting paid.* Saun-tering around the pot of water in the middle of the floor, he glanced up.

"So?" I asked, taking a step closer as I folded my arms.

"You have a leak," he replied, holding a cheeky grin as our eyes met again.

"Ha," I pushed out. This guy might have looked better than Wendy's homemade apple pies, but he was losing my interest fast. Jumping to the point, I asked, "So what's it going to cost me? Still the $550 you quoted me on the phone, I hope?"

He glanced up again and said, "I'll have to check the

extent of the damage, but that's usually what I'd charge for something like this." His eyes met mine. *He sure looks at me a lot.* "But you're a friend of Em's, so I'll do it for $400."

"$400?" I shook my head. *What is it with this town? Everybody just wants to help and give people the best deals.*

He let out a slight chuckle, followed by a shake of his head, as he could see my confusion. "People in this town are good folk. You could learn something from them." He popped an eyebrow up and walked back outside, leaving me with a lingering question. *Learn what, exactly?* Pausing for only a moment as I heard the screen door shut, I decided to follow him.

"When can you get started on this? And how long will it take?" I asked, seeing him go out to his truck. He stopped and shrugged as he turned around, eyeballing the house. "I can order the shingles today and start next Tuesday. It'll take about a day of work unless I discover something different in the full inspection here in a few."

"Great. I have to leave for work here in a minute."

"Okay. I can just come back next week and finish checking it out. It'll delay everything a little bit." He went toward the ladder that was propped up against my roof.

"No. You can just stay and lock up when you're done. Call the diner if you need anything. I'll be there until six."

He nodded and flashed me a trusting smile. Leaving someone at my home unattended worried me some, but Emma knew the people in Newport more than I did, and I trusted her.

I RESTED ONE HAND ON THE MONITOR WHILE THE OTHER ONE typed in my server identification number to clock in. Miley approached, chewing on a piece of gum, and said, "Hey, girl."

"Hey," I replied as I counted my hours up in my head. *Six, nine, four, three . . . Plus today. Thirty.*

"Wendy's talking about cutting hours again," Miley said, jolting me out of my thoughts.

I looked at her. "Seriously?"

She nodded.

I murmured under my breath, "Why not just fire that new girl who just texts and takes a million smoke breaks?"

"Hey," Miley said, pulling me out of my wallowing self-pity.

I looked at her with a raised brow.

She tilted her head back behind her toward the nearly empty diner. "Can you take table five? I need to call my mother to see if she can pick up Gwen."

Peeking over, I saw it was the man from the *Inn at the Lake*, and my heart fluttered. "I knew I knew him from some-where!" Seeing Miley's inquisitive expression, I continued, "I saw that guy at the *Inn at the Lake* a couple of days ago, but I couldn't place him. He's *that* guy."

Miley glanced over her shoulder at him. "Really? Black coffee and toast guy?"

I nodded slowly as I smirked. "Yep." He was a frequent customer, but it wasn't random or a few times a week. It was the same time and day each week that he came in. It had been going on for two years, according to Miley, and nobody ever dared ask him what the deal was. It was strange. We all had our theories around the diner. Miley believed he just liked routine, Wendy suspected he was just crazy, and I, well, I didn't know what to think of it other than that he was cute. I was too busy to really care, but the fact that I saw him outside the diner had me intrigued now. The guy didn't live in Newport, or at least, nobody thought he did since nobody ever saw him outside the diner.

"Go talk to him." Miley nudged me. "You obviously *like* him. It's written all over your face."

Wrapping my apron around my waist and grabbing a pencil from the cup next to the computer, I headed over to the table. Mystery man was reading the daily newspaper he would snatch from the stack on his way in each time he came. As I approached the table, I pulled out my order pad as he lowered his paper.

"Usual?" I asked.

"Yeah." When his eyes met mine for those brief few seconds, I felt a bolt of electricity course over my body. I felt something I hadn't expected, but it didn't matter. He raised the paper back up to continue reading. *He doesn't remember seeing me at the inn?* Tapping my pencil against the pad, I hesitated at the table for a moment as I tried to come up with something more to say because I wanted another glimpse into his eyes. The plan backfired, though. The pen's tapping irritated him, and he lowered his paper back down. "Is there something *more* you need?"

"I saw you . . ." My words stumbled over one another as I attempted to put sentences together while looking into his gorgeous green eyes. "Outside the diner. At the inn? At the lake." I sighed and cleared my throat as I turned red. "Sorry. I saw you at the *Inn at the Lake*."

He grinned and said, "Oh, you're the one who was spying on me. You must know Jody."

"I do. I mean no! I wasn't spying on you." I laughed. "I work there part-time helping out. Jody and I just met the other day, but she's great."

"I hate her," he replied, raising his paper back up to read. *Really?* The awkwardness wrapped itself in the air between us, and I turned and left the table. He called out to me, "I didn't mean that!"

Furrowing my eyebrows, I turned around and went back over to the table. *"What?"*

"I don't *hate* her. She's just . . ." He shook his head. "It doesn't matter. Now I'm stumbling over words." He laughed nervously. "I'm Charlie." Eyes falling to the clip on my apron, he said, "nice to meet you, *Amy.*"

Smiling as I turned red, I nodded. "Nice to meet you, Charlie. You come on Thursdays, right?"

"Every Thursday morning."

"Cool." As the word came off my lips, I immediately felt like a child. *Cool? Are you a teenager?* "I'll get your order in. Was there anything more I could get for you?"

He shook his head. Charlie's eyes stayed on mine, and for the first time in a long time, I didn't feel invisible. I felt like he could see me, something I hadn't felt in years. I knew right then that he wasn't just a passerby in the world, but someone with whom I could feel a connection—one of those rare but marvelous people that stirs a part of your soul that doesn't come alive but once, maybe twice in a lifetime. My prayers began to gravitate toward wisdom to know what to do next. With so much bad in my past, I held a constant fear of meeting someone new today only to repeat the mistakes of my yesterday.

"Okay." Darting away from the table, I felt like a school girl in a cafeteria who just spoke to the most popular boy. *He thinks you were spying on him!* The rest of his visit, we exchanged smiles as I refilled his coffee and we shared glances across the restaurant as I worked. My heart told me we both knew there was something more to each other, but I think we just weren't sure how to handle it. He was cute and left my head spinning.

CHAPTER 6

*A*cool early morning breeze nipped at my bare shoulders two days later on my way out the door to go work at the *Inn at the Lake*. I went back inside and retrieved a sweater. My eye caught a picture of my late mother on the dresser as I put on a red sweater that she had gotten me the Christmas before she passed. My heart longed to see her again, even to just hear her sweet voice once more. But I knew it'd have to wait until the day we reunite in heaven. Her passing was hard, but the regrets I had afterward were harder. I should have visited a bit more, nagged a bit less, and thanked her for all she had done. She wasn't perfect, but she was my mother and I loved her. Though she gave me the advice to stay with John, I believe she would have been proud of all I had achieved after I left John. I imagined my mother playing with my sweet baby, Hope, in heaven. I know she would've been so thrilled to be a grandmother.

After letting the moment slip away, I headed out the door and drove to the inn for a couple of hours of work before I enjoyed my day off. Pulling into the driveway of the inn, I saw Charlie's car. *For not liking Jody, he sure comes*

33

around here a lot. Fumbling in my mind for an excuse, I arrived at the idea that I needed a drink of water and thus, the reason I was going to go in. The real reason, though, was Charlie. He was too mysterious and cute to not want to know more.

Quietly, I went in through the front door of the inn. Jody had told me I could let myself in whenever I needed. Tiptoeing to remain inconspicuous, I glided through the foyer and toward the kitchen. I could hear them around the corner in the kitchen, so I pressed myself up against the wall and lent an ear to listen.

"Charlie, like I've told you before, there is just *nothing* we can do." Jody's words were strained.

"Yeah, I know, Jody. I guess I just expected more."

Hearing him walk the floor of the kitchen toward the foyer—and thus me—I jerked forward and began walking. We almost bumped into each other, and we both sidestepped to the left, then the right.

"Sorry," we both said.

The frown he was carrying from the kitchen hinted at a smile for the moment as our eyes met. His forest green eyes and musky cologne pulled me. When he touched my arms and shifted me to the opposite side so he could get by, a fire ignited inside me. The sensation of his fingers clasping against my skin swept a tidal wave of warmth throughout my body. Being over a year since I was with John, I missed the warmth of another's touch. We both kept walking, but I couldn't help but look back at him. To my joy, he was also looking at me and smiling.

"Amy," Jody said from behind me, pulling my attention away from Charlie as he left out the door. I looked at her as she asked, "What are you doing in here? The flower beds are almost done." She lifted her chin as she peered behind her in the hallway that led into the kitchen, which still held a view of the French doors leading to the outside balcony. "Or did you finish them?"

"I, uh. I was going to go do that now."

"Why'd you come in then?" she questioned.

"I needed a drink," I replied. As Jody went over to the cupboard, my mind drifted back to Charlie. "How do you know Charlie?" I asked.

Pulling a glass from the cupboard, she said, "He's my stepson."

My eyebrows shot up. *Really? Wow.*

"Why's that 'wow'?" she asked, bringing me a cup of water. Taking it from her, I took a drink as I tried to fabricate a response.

Shrugging, I replied, "I don't know."

Jody slowly nodded. "Charles . . . he's a bit difficult, but I love that kid." Her eyes followed my cup as I set it down on the counter. Raising an eyebrow, I knew the look she was giving me. It said, 'I'm not paying you to sit around and drink water.' Taking the cue, I headed out the French doors that led out to the balcony. Spotting Charlie pushing a canoe out onto the water, I stopped at the railing and watched. He didn't have a shirt on, even though the air was still chilly outside that morning, but I wasn't about to run down there and tell him to put one on. His defined shoulders and unclothed torso reminded me again of how long it had been since I had the close touch of a man. I missed the comfort of a man's arms around me in the form of a hug. Those feelings of being protected and cherished were but a *very* distant memory. Memories that were tucked away under layers and years of abuse, worry and anxiety. Seeing Charlie made me begin to wonder how Charlie's arms around me would make me feel. Could he bring me those once familiar feelings? My mind soon drifted elsewhere as I admired his body. *This is a sin,* I told myself, breaking my concentration off the hunky eye candy. Continuing to the end of the balcony, I headed down to start in on the flower beds.

———

AFTER FINISHING A GRUELING MORNING OF WORK IN THE flower beds, I realized on my way home I had forgotten my sweater on the railing of the upper balcony. Sweater or no sweater, I wasn't going back to Jody's. I had a handful of errands to run, as it was my only day off. After finishing everything around town I needed to do, I had plans for a night that was going to consist of reruns of General Hospital and bonbons—a new favorite treat of mine.

After a hot shower and slipping into a pair of pajamas, I curled up on the couch to watch my show when the doorbell rang. My heart pounded as I gripped my couch pillow. Though it had been a year, I still worried about John finding me. Glancing at my phone, I saw it was eight o'clock.

The knock came again.

Setting the pillow to my side, I reached under the couch and grabbed my can of pepper spray as a precaution. Holding it behind my back, I stood up and headed to the door. My heart pounded as I approached the door and peered through the peephole to see who it was.

Charlie.

I breathed a sigh of relief and swung open the door, slipping the pepper spray onto the entryway table out of sight. Grasping the edge of the door, I said, "Charlie."

A sideways smile from the corner of his lip revealed his awkward feelings about being on my porch. He tossed a thumb over his shoulder to his car. "I have your sweater. I brought it." His eyes traced my Tweety Bird pajamas, and I felt my cheeks flush. *Ugh! I can't believe I'm wearing this.*

"Oh, neat. Yeah. Thanks . . ." Raising my eyebrows, I glanced over to his car.

He laughed nervously. "Sorry I didn't bring it up to the porch. I don't know why I didn't do that." He shook his head. "Let me go get it."

He turned and jogged down the porch steps and across the gravel to his car. I stepped out onto the porch. Watching as he fumbled through his car, I scanned the perimeter out of habit after having a scare. It was something I did daily after first moving to town, but it became less and less often over the course of the last year. Seeing him pull my red sweater out and holding it up near the car, I smiled. Charlie walked back over and came up to meet me on the porch.

"I came back over to Jody's to talk to her and saw the sweater on the railing. Figured I'd bring it by."

"How'd you know where I lived?" I asked.

"Jody."

Since this guy made the decision to bring my sweater to me, unannounced and after eight at night, I decided to ask, "Why don't you like her?"

He handed me the sweater and slowly shook his head. "It's a long story."

"I've got time."

He pursed his lips and squinted as he tried to figure me out or something. His green eyes looked me over. "Well . . ." He let out a sigh. "It's just . . . *family* drama."

An eyebrow went up as I replied, "Yeah? What kind of *family* drama, if I may ask?"

"Nothing really. Jody was married to my dad before he passed away, and now she wants to sell his boat down at the marina."

"Doesn't seem like that long of story," I said with a playful smile. Not knowing what else to say without being intrusive, I rubbed the corner of my sweater's hem and waited for him to say something more about it. He began to look uncomfortable as he adjusted his footing and leaned onto the railing behind him. I went to stop him, but it was too late.

Crack! The railing gave way and broke, sending Charlie flailing, arms and all, along with the whole rickety railing, toppling over to the flower bed below. Darting down the steps, I hurried down to him. Dropping to my knees beside my wounded deliverer, I asked, "Are you all right?"

Grabbing his head as he went beet-red, he flashed a quick nod. He got up in a hurry and brushed off the dirt from his jeans. "I'm sorry. I'm going to fix this."

"No," I replied. "That's okay. I'll get it taken care of."

Raising a hand, he said, "I insist. I came over without even a phone call and smashed your porch up. Let me take care of this." His pleading eyes and sweet smile were hard to resist, but I did.

"Don't worry about it. It was already falling apart and needed repaired. I'm pretty handy with a hammer and nails." Noticing a cut above his eyebrow, I said, "You're bleeding. Come inside and let me clean that cut up."

"I have to get going."

I raised an eyebrow as I realized I didn't even know if this guy was single. "Wife or something waiting at home?"

"*Something?*" He laughed. "Just a needy house cat is all. She gets mad when I'm gone from the house too long." He looked back at his car and then at my house. Feeling his forehead with a few fingers, he found the trickle of blood running down the side of his face. "Oh, wow. I guess it's bleeding pretty good."

"Come inside." I tilted my head toward the porch, and he followed behind me. As we walked up the porch and headed through the front door, it dawned on me that I hadn't had a male in my house in the last year. Not in a non-professional manner, anyway.

As he sat down at the kitchen table, I dampened a wash rag in the sink. Looking back at him, I asked, "Where do you work?"

"Ikan Web Designs in Spokane. I'm a graphic designer."

"You like it?" I asked, glancing at him as I grabbed the Band-Aids from the cupboard.

"It's a good job. I'm looking to branch off on my own soon, though. Go global. Be my own boss and work out of my house. I think something like that would be amazing." Catching another glimpse of him, I saw his eyes light up at the talk of starting his own business venture. *Ambitious. I like that.* Finding a Band-Aid that would do the job, I set the box back in the cupboard and walked over to the table.

"Why haven't you done it?" I asked.

He shrugged.

I nodded slowly as I began to gently dab the blood off his forehead.

His tone soft, he said, "I've always got an excuse for why I don't start doing it. I . . ."

My eyes met his as I pulled the wash rag away from his face. He looked hesitant to continue, so I pressed. "What, Charlie?"

"I'm scared of failing." He let out a breath of air like a relief valve. He continued, "Huh. I never realized that before." He watched me as I peeled the wrappings away from the Band-Aid and then asked, "So what's *your* deal, Amy? Where'd you come from before Dixie's diner?"

Rippling memories from my past came rushing to the forefront of my mind, crippling the enjoyable moment. *Why'd he have to go there?* I sighed. "New York," I replied curtly. There wasn't any harm in giving that up to him, and my hope was that he'd drop it. *I guess that's what I get for trying to figure him out.* "Have you always lived around here? Around Newport?" I asked, hoping to divert him.

"I know what you're doing. Don't try to redirect the focus off yourself, Amy. Tell me. What were you doing in New York City?"

"*State.* Not City. Um . . . Just living and whatnot." I placed the Band-Aid over his wound, and my mind continued the conversation where my lips did not. *And by living, I mean being beat by a man that I had to run away from and go clear across the country to save myself and my baby. Then I lost the baby and almost ended my life. But I didn't, thanks to God. After recommitting my life to the Lord, I'm now living by a secret name and trying to pretend my abusive husband doesn't exist! And I can't ask for a divorce or he'd find me! Eek!* Too bad I didn't have the courage to tell him.

"Living and whatnot . . . huh." He raised an eyebrow and touched his forehead where the Band-Aid was now securely fastened. I could tell in his tone and his eyes that he knew there was something more to my story, but he didn't push it. "Thanks for this."

"Oh, it's nothing."

"No, really. Thank you. It's not every day that I have a pretty woman taking care of me."

I beamed. His words were like sweet honey to my ears if they had taste buds—delicious. Feeling drawn to him, I wanted to know more about his life. "What about that boat of your dad's? Why is *that* the beef between you and your mom?"

"She's not my mother, for one." He stood up, making eye contact with me with those fierce green eyes. I took in a whiff of his scent as he continued, "And for two—I don't want to talk about it. I get the feeling you with your 'living and whatnot' in New York don't mind not discussing certain things."

"I'd love that," I said with a bit more enthusiasm than I should have had.

He flashed me a pearly white smile, heading for the front door.

"See you Thursday?" I blurted out.

He looked back at me and said, "See you Thursday."

As the door shut, I caught myself smiling, and it worried me. *Am I really ready to pursue a relationship with someone?* The idea of dating again was laughable. Awkward long pauses at the front door, wondering if he'd kiss me. *Ugh.* When I had laid out my plan for my new life, I never dreamed of adding a new relationship to the mix. My assumption was that I'd never love again, but that was a bit dramatic. I knew I wanted kids and a family *someday*, just not sure when. John was a jerk. It'd be easy for me to fall in love, and I was scared of that. My eyes drifted to Milo as he leaped onto the entertainment stand and made himself comfortable in front of the TV. Pulling back the curtain that draped over the living room window, I watched as Charlie got into his car.

The walls I had built up around me over the last year weren't coming down, but they were definitely feeling a bit weaker in spots.

CHAPTER 7

*A*rriving at Dixie's the following Monday, I checked my phone after feeling it buzz in my pocket on the drive in. Checking to see who it was, I was pleasantly surprised to see it was Joe. He had received the shingles a day early and had time to start work on the roof that afternoon.

ME: GREAT! IF YOU NEED TO GO INSIDE AT ALL, JUST LET **yourself in with the key that's under the clay tortoise on the porch.**

Joe: Ha-ha. Why even lock your door if you just leave a key hidden in a place that obvious?

Me: Never thought of it that way. Heading into work now. See you around three when I'm off work.

WITH A SPRING IN MY STEP, I WENT INSIDE AND CLOCKED IN for my shift. The restaurant was beginning to get busy as the usual morning patrons began showing up. Refilling coffees, delivering plates of food, and talking about the latest bear attack with the locals filled most the early parts of my shift. To my surprise, Frank and Sue came in around eleven thirty.

"Pretty early for you two," I said, greeting them as I approached their table. "Going to have some breakfast?"

"No," Sue replied. "We're just having an early lunch. The usual will be fine. You sure do look lovely today, Amy. Did you get a haircut?"

Raising an eyebrow, I replied, "Nope. Just in a good mood."

"You do have a certain glow to you," Frank added.

"I did find out I'm getting my roof repaired today," I replied, jotting down their usual order of meatloaf and potatoes on my order pad. "Things are just going *really* good right now."

"Good," Frank said.

Walking back through the restaurant, I dwelled on the term Frank used—glow. I touched my cheek as I walked up to the server window, and Diego asked, "What's going on with your cheek?"

Peering over my shoulder in the direction of Frank and Sue, I said, "Frank told me I have a glow."

"You do seem happy today," Diego replied, snatching an order slip from a clip. His eyes ran over the piece of paper for a moment, and then he set it aside and turned around to the flat top. *What does a glow even mean, really?* My mind wandered to the last time I saw Charlie sitting at my table. I smiled. He was getting to me more than I was letting myself realize.

"Amy," Wendy said with a stern voice from the corner that wrapped down a hallway to the back. Raising my eyebrows, I jerked my head to her, giving my full attention. "Did you serve a woman a ginger ale the other day when she asked for an iced tea?"

Fumbling through my mind and tables, I didn't recall the incident. "No."

She squinted with suspicious eyes as she looked me over. "Okay . . ." Glancing to the front door, she continued, "Let Miley know to come see me when she gets in."

AFTER WORK, I ARRIVED HOME NOT ONLY TO JOE'S TRUCK, BUT Charlie's car in my driveway. Then, in front of my house, stood the two fully-grown men arguing and shouting at one another. Seeing the situation escalate between them, I parked quickly and rushed across the gravel over to the two of them.

"What on earth is going on?" I asked, seeing Joe with a trickle of blood dripping from his nose.

Joe shot a nod in Charlie's direction and said, "Why don't you ask lover boy here?" Walking past me, he headed to his truck and said, "Let me know when he's not here, and I'll finish the job." The slam of his driver's side door made me cringe.

I raised my eyebrows as I saw Charlie with a grimace. Staring at Joe, I asked, "What happened?"

Joe's truck started, and he peeled out of the driveway in reverse, kicking rocks up in a fury as he tore out of the driveway. *I'm probably going to get stuck with full-price now.*

"A disagreement. That's all." Charlie turned and went over to the porch, where I saw a few freshly installed two-by-fours already secured in place while a pile of others sat on the ground in front of the flower bed.

"I'll ask again—what happened?" I asked, following behind him.

Charlie turned around and looked me in the eyes. He looked not only upset, but reluctant. Letting out a sigh, he cleared his throat and said smoothly, "Joe Dilasky and I went to high school together . . . and well, we just have an old beef."

I couldn't help but laugh. "And what? You tried to settle it with him in front of my house?"

"*No.* I didn't even bring anything up. It was so long ago. I just went about what I was doing, but he brought it up and started going off about it." Charlie picked up a two-by-four and his hammer and walked over to the porch.

"So you hit him because he was talking to you?" I asked. Though the details might have not been important to most people, they were to me. Violence was a touchy subject due to my history with John, and if I was taking an interest in the same type of man, I needed to know.

"No. When I didn't respond to him, he began pushing me and even shoved me over. I snapped and knocked him in the face with a good punch."

"You solved the problem with violence—cool." My eyes rolled, and my interest began dwindling with that one choice he made.

"Look—I didn't start it. He's a jerk, and I don't like him. I defended myself."

Nodding, I said, "Whatever. I need to go inside and change."

Walking past him, I went up the porch steps and stopped before I went inside. I looked back at him. His eyes met mine, and I saw him in a different light in that moment. He reminded me too much of someone I ran away from, someone I wanted nothing to do with anymore. I turned and went inside. There was no way I was going to put up with behaviors like that from another guy. It reminded me too much of John, and I wasn't interested in becoming another punching bag for someone who used violence to work through their problems in life. Dropping my keys on the entryway table, I headed through the living room toward the hallway. Letting my palm run along Milo's back, I whispered, "At least I have *you*."

The sound of Charlie's hammer clanged in my ears for the next hour. I didn't go back out to see him. I went about my usual afternoon activities. I put in a load of wash, washed the few dishes in the sink from that morning, and talked to my cat as I caught up on my reading. For a moment, I thought he'd left as the hammer sounds stopped. Standing up from the couch, I went over and peeked out the curtain to see if he did. Unfortunately for me, he was not only there but caught my glance. When he waved me to come outside, I was reluctant to do so but decided to be nice.

"Yeah?" I asked as I stepped out onto the porch, Milo following me. Milo stretched out as he pawed at the porch's wood planks. Catching Charlie smile as he looked at Milo, I felt annoyed. Wrestling against my own lingering feelings of interest for Charlie, I adjusted my footing and crossed my arms, trying to hide it.

"I'm really sorry about Joe. That's not like me." He shrugged and glanced back toward the driveway and then back at me. "I don't know what came over me." He let out a sigh.

"What is it Joe did?"

"If you must know, it's not what he did . . ."

I raised an eyebrow as I looked at him. "Go on."

He let out a soft laugh and rubbed his jaw, then said, "Well, it's simple . . . just a little silly. I stole his prom date for our senior prom."

"Wow . . . and he's *still* mad about that?"

He laughed. "I guess. Honestly, I was just defending myself, Amy."

I dropped my arms to my sides as I struggled to realize that Charlie was defending himself, something I always longed to be able to do. I needed to give him the benefit of the doubt and pray about it. *I can't just write someone off imme-diately because of the slightest reminder of John.* Smiling, I shook my head and looked at him. "To be honest with you, Charlie, between smashing up my porch and beating up my roofer, I'm starting to—"

"Not like me?" he replied with a laugh. "I get it. Just keep diggin' that hole for myself."

I laughed. "You really are digging quite the hole."

His eyes fell to the almost completed railing, and he glanced over at me. "Give me another shot?"

Raising an eyebrow, I asked, "What do you have in mind?"

"Dinner. Movie." He held his eyebrows up and focused on me, waiting for a reply. The silent and mysterious guy was opening up a bit more than I ever expected. He went from the coffee and two pieces of toast guy to Charlie Dillard, the kind-hearted entrepreneur and master hole-digger.

"All right, but no movie. I hate how people think movies are great. They don't give you any time to talk. Dinner and a walk would be nice, though."

"Little bossy, aren't ya?" Charlie asked.

"I know what I want—that's all."

"I like that. I'll pick you up, and we'll go into Spokane. When is a good time for you?"

Thinking about it for a moment, I tapped my lips as I thought and answered, "Friday evening would be good. How's eight?"

He smiled and said, "It's a date." Going over to the wood, he picked up another two-by-four and continued working on the porch railing.

Pressing on my mind out of nowhere came a question. "Where do you live?" I blurted out.

He stopped and looked over at me. "Down the road from the inn. Why?"

"Why doesn't anyone ever see you in town?"

He laughed. "I don't know. I buy most my stuff in Spokane, and I prefer to be at home. You okay?"

Smiling at him, I nodded. "I'll see you for our date." I turned and went inside. Peering through my living room window again, I watched him go back to work on the railing. As I looked out, I prayed that God would give me the wisdom to know if this one was bad news. There was no way I could put up with another John in my lifetime.

CHAPTER 8

Three days passed, and Thursday morning, I found myself awake before the sun was up. Slumber wouldn't come to me during the night as I wrestled with my emotions over the impending date with Charlie tomorrow. *Was it okay to go on a date when I haven't even been officially divorced from John?* Leaving my struggle beneath my comforter on my bed, I decided to get ready and go over to the *Inn at the Lake*. My hopes were to catch the sunrise and get a couple of hours of work in before heading into Dixie's Diner.

As I walked down the path to the water at the inn, the sun was already beginning to come up over the treetops. Vibrant pinks, purples and reds lit the morning sky, reminding me how beautiful God's paint strokes truly were. *He's always near.*

Stepping off the path, I walked through the grass and over to the dock. The waters were still and undisturbed. Silence wrapped itself around me and brought a calmness to my soul as I took in not only the sunrise, but God's nature all around. Walking the length of the dock, I came to the end and stood.

Pine trees filled most of the scenery around the lake, with the only exception being houses, but there weren't many of those either.

"Tranquil, isn't it?" Emma said from behind me, causing me to jump a little.

Turning around, I said, "Sorry. You scared me. I didn't know anyone was down here or awake this time of day."

She smiled warmly as she walked down the dock to me. A robe wrapped around her thin frame and her messy hair gave the indication she'd stayed the night at the inn.

"Did you stay here last night?" I asked.

"I did." She let out a wistful sigh before continuing. "Jody's husband, Wayne, isn't doing well, and I stayed over to discuss the future. Just family stuff. What are you doing out here so early in the morning?"

"I couldn't sleep." Hesitation stopped me from explaining, but she seemed to already know.

"Charlie?" she said.

"Yes," I replied. "How did you . . . ?"

"Things have a way of getting around."

Nodding, my eyes turned back to the water. Seeing a fish jump, my eyes traced the ripples.

Touching her lips with a couple of fingers, Emma looked out at the water and pointed. "My husband, when he was still with us, used to fish this lake with our boy, Lenny. They'd sit out in that boat for hours. I caught Lenny, on more than one occasion, praying at the kitchen table for God to let him catch a bigger fish than his dad." A deep smile set into Emma's face as she looked over at me with tear-filled eyes. Grasping onto my arm, she said, "Don't ever give up on hope for the future, for love, for healing and for life. For *hope* is what connects us to God. Lenny hoped to catch a bigger fish than his father, but you hoped to have a new life when you moved here, Serenah. You just have to choose to live with hope and not be crippled by the fear of the past."

I smiled as Emma's words touched the depths of my soul. She was right. I needed to stop letting the fear of John rule my life. It was over a year ago, and I needed to press on and enjoy the new life I had created in Newport. Charlie wasn't John. My worry over the date tomorrow evening with Charlie soon dwindled.

"I have a gift for you," Emma said. "Come with me."

She led me off the dock, across the grass by the shore, and over to the thicket of trees that lined the property. We weaved through a few trees until an opening where a patch of dirt lay with a baby pine tree. "What is this?" I asked as I approached the small tree and crouched, letting my finger-tips fall across the pine needles that adorned the branches.

"It's your tree. It's for the memory of your baby girl."

Tears instantly welled in my eyes. I had expressed my grievance to her over the fact I had no burial plot or memorial for Hope. Smiling, I stood up and wrapped my arms around her neck. "Thank you so much."

"I knew the anniversary of her loss was coming up, and—"

"You're truly the sweetest person I've ever met," I said as tears trickled down my cheeks. It warmed my heart that she cared so much about me. Turning toward the lake that was visible through the trees, I said, "It's a beautiful view of the lake for Hope."

"It is. She deserves to have a memorial, Serenah. She changed your life for the better."

I smiled and wiped the tears from my eyes as I nodded. "I can't thank you enough." We continued to visit for a while longer before I headed back over to start in on more yard work.

As I weeded near one of the tall standing pine trees in the

front yard near the driveway, a black Lexus RC pulled into the driveway of the inn. *That looks just like John's,* I thought to myself. My heart began pounding, and I moved to the shrubs out of view. Watching as it pulled up, I hid further into the shrubs, pushing against sharp twigs and branches. The car pulled further ahead, and my sights fell onto Washington state plates, settling my nerves. *When am I ever going to shake this fear?* The car rolled to a stop, and a woman got out. Turning, I went back to weeding near the pine trees in the front.

Biting on her nails, Miley looked a bit nervous when I showed up at the diner at nine. She didn't take her eyes off the front door the entire time I clocked in. "You're acting strange," I commented as I wrapped my apron around my waist.

Dropping her hand from her mouth, she turned to me. Lowering her voice as she leaned in, she said, "Wendy drilled into me the other day about some stupid customer who got a lemonade instead of an iced tea."

"Ginger ale."

Miley paused and pulled her head back. "Wait. You knew?"

"Knew what? I knew there was a problem with someone's order."

"And you threw me under the bus?" Miley retorted.

"Um . . . No. She asked if it was me, and I said *no.*" Placing a pencil behind my ear, I said, "Why does she act like she's just waiting to fire us all?"

"Right?" Miley replied, shaking her head. "Why does Emma let her treat us like that?"

I shrugged. "I'm sure it has to do with the fact that Emma co-owns the diner with Debbie, and Debbie's her aunt."

"Ahh . . . yeah. Nepotism at its finest."

"Order up," Diego said from the server window a few steps away.

Miley flashed Diego a nod and headed that way, but not without saying on the way, "Lover boy should be here soon."

My heart dipped at Charlie's mention. Glancing at the computer screen, I saw he was due to come in any moment. Pushing a loose strand of hair behind my ear, I smiled and took a deep breath.

The door chimed, and in walked Charlie. Turning around, our eyes connected, and though we both smiled, I felt something in the air that he brought in with him. It wasn't good. The feeling reminded me of the mysterious no-named man I had seen come in on Thursdays for months—but different. He looked grieved, and his shoulders sagged as he went to a table and sat down. Walking across the diner, I decided to play it easy, see if he'd divulge what was going on.

"Hey, Charlie."

He looked up from his paper and tipped his chin, forced half-smile and all. "Amy."

"Usual?" I asked, wanting to know more about this little thing he did. Today wasn't the day to push it, though. I could tell that much.

He let out a sigh and said, "Yes. The usual." As I wrote it down and turned to walk away, he called my name.

"Amy."

Turning around, I looked at him.

He hesitated for a moment and shook his head. "Never mind."

Not able to stand it another moment, I shoved the order pad in my apron and went over to him. Resting my hands on the table, I asked, "What's going on in that head of yours, Charlie?"

He appeared to mull something over in his mind, and then he looked at me in a way that cut through all my layers and walls and into my soul. He asked, "You ever just have some days that are just a little bit harder than the rest?"

I nodded, thinking about the anniversary of my baby's death being just two days away—Saturday. "Absolutely."

"Yeah. It's just one of *those* days."

Bringing a hand up to his shoulder, I touched him and smoothed my thumb gently, giving him comfort. With a soft voice, I said, "I understand. I'll get your order in." As I cut through the restaurant, I thought more about my baby girl that never lived outside my womb. Often, I wondered if I would have been a good mom. Part of me used to feel God had made me miscarry because He didn't think I'd be a good one. Luckily, though, my time at counseling taught me otherwise. Peering back at Charlie as he was weighed down with whatever was bothering him, I felt myself slip a bit further into having deeper feelings for him.

Those walls didn't stand a chance.

CHAPTER 9

The flame of the candle in the center of the table flickered as a warm evening breeze blew through the patio of the restaurant in downtown Spokane. Raising my hand to catch my hair in the breeze, I pushed strands behind my ear and smiled at Charlie as he sat across from me. His smile glowed in the light of the candle. He had a nice suit and tie on, and his scent was especially intoxicating tonight. Though we didn't talk about whatever was weighing him down yesterday at the diner, we did learn a lot about each other's quirky histories and he kept me laughing through most the night.

"I can't believe you've *never* have had a s'more before," he said with a laugh before proceeding to finish his last bite of chocolate cake. "You were *such* a sheltered child!"

Shooing a playful hand gesture out in front of me, I let out a laugh. "Oh, come on! I haven't been *that* sheltered. I sneaked out when I was sixteen once."

"Yeah . . . What'd you do?" He crossed his arms as his eyebrows went up and he leaned back in his seat.

"My friend, Chelsea, and I slept in her car."

He folded over as he let out a laugh. "Slept in the car? Ooh. Risky." Composing himself after another few moments of laughing, he settled down. He took a deep breath before smiling and looking me in the eyes. "You're too cute, Amy. You know that?"

Calling me by my fake name brought reality crashing back into my world in an instant. I was so caught up in the evening and enjoying our time together that all the realities of my deception were suspended, and we were just two souls enjoying the evening together. *I wish he knew my real name.* Forcing a smile, I said, "Yeah? Cute?"

"Yeah," he replied. Pausing for a moment, he gripped the arms of the chair suddenly and leaned in over the table. "You want to get out of here? Go for a walk in Riverfront Park?" He glanced over his shoulder at the moon and said, "Moonlight walk down by the falls?"

Without speaking a word, I looked into his eyes and saw the depths of his soul. He was happy—at least, in this moment, he was. Being the one responsible for bringing that warmth to his eyes filled me with joy. Though I wasn't telling Charlie everything, I knew what was developing was real. And while I did love John once before, I never felt like just being with me was ever good enough for him. There always had to be something more going on—a movie, dancing, gambling, whatever. There was no such thing as 'going for a walk' with my John. Even those trips to the city were riddled with activities to stay busy.

My heart was moving fast with Charlie, but I couldn't stop it. Every passing moment surpassed the moment before.

As we walked one of the bridges in Riverfront Park

holding hands, he stopped and turned to me. "That boat is the only thing left of my dad."

Bouncing between his eyes, I saw how much it meant to him. Worry and hurt hid behind his green eyes. "I'm sorry. There isn't anything you can do?"

He shook his head and his chin dipped to his chest. "She said she's going to sell it because she's tired of paying the $250 a month to dry dock it and making sure its upkeep is all good. She's just done. I can't afford that kind of money right now, so she wants to sell it. I mean . . . I get it. It's a lot of money to shell out for a boat, but it was *my* dad's boat. Jody met my father ten years ago, and they were deeply in love when he passed in a tragic car accident a couple of years back. I guess between her marrying Wayne and now wanting to get rid of the boat . . . I feel like maybe she never really loved my dad." He bit his lip and turned away as his eyes began to glisten by the obviously painful words he spoke. Walking over to the cement railing of the bridge, he stretched his arms out and grasped onto the edge with both hands. That invisible weight that I had seen yesterday at the diner appeared to be back on his shoulders.

Walking up to his side, I placed a hand on his back, and he looked into my eyes.

"It's the last thing I have of *his* in this world, Amy." His eyes turned away and to the rushing falls beyond the railing. The sound of the crashing water took over the silence in the air between us. Not sure what to do or say, I just stood by his side, keeping my hand on his back. After a few minutes, he said, "I don't really share this kind of thing with many people. I'm sorry if I came across all . . . I don't know. All emotional or something."

I grabbed his hand and looked at him. "I love getting to know more about you. You can share anything with me."

"Same goes for you," he replied.

A smile grew from the corner of his lips as he threaded his fingers into mine and we continued our walk. We continued talking and enjoying the quiet summer evening as we walked around Riverfront Park. When we crossed the street back over to the car after our walk, I noticed another black Lexus RC parked a few parking spaces from Charlie's car. *Is that the same one from the inn?* Unable to see the plates in the dark, I got in and soon forgot about it as Charlie's gaze in my direction stole my attention.

"Hi," I said, smiling as I looked into his eyes.

"Hi."

Seeing him steal a glance at my lips, I said, "Could we avoid the weird porch thing where I pretend to fumble around for my keys and just get our first kiss out of the way right now?"

He laughed. "Way to kill the romantic suspense of the evening, Amy." He adjusted in his seat so he was partially over the armrest, leaning toward me. "You really do know what you want."

"Well, I'm just—"

He interrupted me by coming the rest of the way over the armrest and pulling my head toward him for a kiss. When his lips pressed against mine, it was as if a release valve blew and pressure began releasing. A deep warmth ran from my head, reaching down all the way into my toes and bathing my body in a bath of warming passion. Pressing against his direction as we kissed, the warmth pulsed within my chest. I could feel my heart beat harder and harder as the warmth grew inside me. I grabbed onto his jacket and slid it off his shoulders. His muscular shoulders and arms revealed themselves in the low lighting that shone in from the street lamp outside. All boundaries fell away in my mind as I looked him in the eyes. Dipping my head, I kissed him deeper as I began climbing over to his seat.

He grabbed onto my arms and gently pushed me back, making me want him even more. A serious look flashed across his face, and he said, "*Amy . . .*"

I bit my lip and dove back toward him across the armrest, but he resisted. Pushing me back again, he let out a laugh and then a groan.

"Calm down, babe. We can't let this get carried away."

I reluctantly relaxed back into my seat and looked over at him as my emotions began to calm back down. I was frustrated but thankful for his ability to control himself. He was sweet, far sweeter than any of the men I'd ever dealt with in my life. "Thank you," I said softly before directing my eyes forward through the windshield. Sliding his jacket back on, he reached over and grabbed my hand, threading his fingers between mine.

"I care about you too much to mess up what we have," he said. "That probably doesn't sound right."

I smiled. "It does." The temptation was there for both of us, but we knew it wasn't right.

Putting the car into drive, Charlie drove us back toward Newport. On the drive back, I started wondering why he would resist me. *It has to be his faith or moral compass of some sort.* Finally getting up the nerve, I asked, "Are you a Christian?"

"Yes. I'm a Biblical born-again Christian. You?" he asked, looking over at me.

My heart clung to that sweet response. "Yes. Where do you go to church?"

"Pines Baptist in the Valley. You?"

"Foursquare on the South Hill. You been going all your life?"

He nodded. The street lights on the freeway glinted through the car's windows as we drove, allowing me to catch small images of his gorgeous face. Charlie made me not only feel safe, but cared for and adored like a precious gem. I could spend hours with him and love every moment of it. Unable to wipe the smile from my face, I felt happy, relaxed and at peace the whole ride back to town despite the slight rejection I felt.

AFTER ROUNDING THE EVENING OFF WITH A FEW MORE KISSES on my porch and almost breaking the railing a second time, Charlie headed home. Going inside, I couldn't stop myself from smiling. It continued through the living room as I told Milo, "You should be worried. It might not just be me and you forever." My grin didn't even stop as I went down the hallway and into my bedroom to change out of my clothing and into pajamas. As I put lotion on my arms in front of my vanity mirror, I saw the glow Frank had mentioned. My heart was happy, and joy warmed throughout my body. *He's seriously amazing . . . Thank you, God.*

A hard knock came from the front door. Smiling, I thought, *he must have decided he needed another kiss.* As I made my way out to the living room, the knock came again. "Hold on, I'm coming . . ."

Not bothering to check the peephole, I opened the door, and it was if somebody threw a sack of bricks at my face. I slammed it as quickly as possible upon seeing that it was John. I pressed my back against the door as I began to hyper-ventilate. Turning around, I quickly locked the door and began to think of what to do as I scanned my living room. *Stay calm! Stay calm!*

"C'mon, *Serenah*. It's me, John. I'm not drinking anymore."

Seeing the pepper spray on the entryway table beside me, I grabbed it and put my finger on the trigger. Still with the door locked, I stalled. "Since when?"

"I'm a year sober."

"Cute. You waited for me to leave to sober up? How *sweet*."

"Can you open the door so we can chat?"

Grasping the pepper spray, I shook my head as I shouted through the locked door. "No. I don't think that's a good idea."

No reply.

Suddenly, a sound came from another part of the house. Realizing I had left my bedroom window open earlier to air out the house, I sprinted through the living room and down the hallway. Holding out my can of pepper spray, I went into the bedroom. Seeing his torso halfway through the window, I said, "Stop! I'll . . . I'll spray you!"

He looked up at me and pushed back his hair as it fell partially into his eyes. Smiling, he said, "Honey, put that down." He came the rest of the way through the window and fell onto the hardwood floor.

"John, just get out of here! I'm going to call the cops."

He stood up, raising his hands. "Don't spray me with that, and please, don't call the cops. I just want to talk. I want to get back together."

"Breaking into my house after I said 'no' to *chat* with you isn't a good way of convincing me."

He laughed and scanned the room. "So what? You move across the country and find a beater little project house to work on while you try to forget me?" His eyes fell back onto mine. Flashes of our life together came boiling to the surface, the good mixed in with the bad. "I found the pregnancy test, *Serenah*." He glanced past me and said, "Where's my child?"

Pressing my lips together to form a thin line, my eyes welled with tears. "I miscarried her at fifteen weeks."

Bringing his hands to his face, he folded his eyes into his palms and began weeping. It wasn't a side I'd ever seen of

John. Unsure of what to do, I kept the can of pepper spray pointed at him. After a few moments, he wiped tears from his now red eyes. His lips quivered as he asked, "Was it because of me?"

"Not directly. Stress induced. It was too much for my body. How'd you find me, John?" Tears glistened in my eyes as I stood trembling with the spray in my hands.

"My private investigator found your phony P.O. box in Seattle. That was cute, but not how I ultimately found you. It was your social security number." He sighed. "You know, Serenah . . . I found a positive pregnancy test in the garbage can the day after you left. Do you have any idea what that did to me? To *know* you were carrying *my* baby and ran?" He took a step toward me, but a flash of him backhanding me in our past surfaced.

"Stay away from me!" I shouted, jerking the can of pepper spray toward him.

He held up his hands. "I'll leave." He went over to the window and climbed out. Pausing, he said, "One day, you'll be back in my arms. We can make another baby, honey. Think about it." Dropping into the darkness, he left.

The curtains at the window flapped in the breeze as I waited a moment to make sure he was gone. Hearing the car door shut somewhere off in the distance outside, I hurried across the floor and slammed the window shut, locking it. Then, I quickly ran throughout the house, making sure everything was locked. After finishing the last check on the window in the living room, I collapsed into a puddle of tears on the floor.

My worst nightmare had come true—he had found me.

CHAPTER 10

$\mathcal{T}$he next day wasn't one I was looking forward to—the anniversary of my baby girl's death. My heart pounded as I drove to the inn to visit Hope's memorial tree and read her the letter that I had written last night. I had awoken in the wee hours of the morning thinking about her and was unable to fall back asleep. Spilling my heart onto a piece of notebook paper I had found on the nightstand, I told my baby girl just how I felt. The anticipation of reading aloud the epitaph was almost too much to handle when coupled with the fact that John was in town. Much of my life didn't make sense, but the loss of my child was, by far, the most painful experience I had ever endured. The event of losing Hope surpassed all the beatings that John had ever made me endure.

Getting out with a bundle of daises in one hand that I had bought on my way and the letter in the other, I walked around the house and down toward the woods. The quietness of the early morning set me at ease as I entered the woods. Though it was still early in the day, the air had already begun to feel warm as a breeze blew my skirt and flowers. *Where's her tree?* My eyes jumped from tree to tree as I walked deeper into the woods that separated the properties.

There.

Finding it was good, and yet, a kind of misery settled over me at the same time. Sadness and joy were woven together so tightly in my heart that I couldn't tell where one ended and the other began. My forefront emotion was joy that layered itself with the sadness underneath. Though she had died, Hope had helped me so much. She'd helped me escape John and the abuse he inflicted on my life, my existence. If it wasn't for her, I would've never made the decision to go to counseling. It was through that experience that I learned to become a strong woman of God. The loss of my baby had been used by God to shape me into who He wanted me to be.

Though there was never a day that went by without her crossing my mind, there were plenty of moments in which I'd tried to avoid the fact that Hope ever existed.

I felt guilty over that.

Taking a deep breath, I set the flowers down and leaned them against the tree and then unfolded the piece of notebook paper. Tears fell onto the paper and my bottom lip began to tremble. Pulling in my lip, I bit it and then took another deep breath. *You can do this.* I began reading aloud the letter I wrote.

I will never get to see you grow,
Kiss your tiny fingers or your toes.
Though I will never get to see you smile,
I love that you grew inside me for a while.
This tree is a memory for you, my baby girl.
Though you're not here, you changed my whole world.
You'll always be alive in my heart,
In spirit and love, though we be apart.

It's because of you I found courage to do what is right.
It's because of you I found strength within myself to fight.
It's because of you I found God in the midst of strife.
It's because of you I found love, and in turn, a new life.

Though I will never see you grow,
Kiss your tiny fingers and your toes.
Though I will never get to see you smile,
I love that you grew inside me for a while.
This tree is a memory for you, my baby girl.
Though you're not here, you changed my whole world.

STEPPING CLOSER TO THE TREE, I GOT DOWN ON MY HANDS and knees and folded the note back up. Pulling loose dirt away from the ground near the tree, I buried the letter. *I love you, Hope. I will always love you.*

"Amy?" a man's voice said from not far away, somewhere behind me in the distance.

Turning around, I was surprised to see Charlie walking through the woods. *What do I tell him?* My heart began to race as he raised his eyebrows, coming closer as I stood up. Making it over to me, he touched my arm and tilted his head. "What's wrong?"

Pulling in my bottom lip, I bit it as I worried what to say. Then letting it go, I told him, "I had a daughter I miscarried at fifteen weeks a year ago today. Emma planted this tree in memorial of her for me."

Shaking his head, he looked at me and said, "Wow. I couldn't imagine what that must be like. Sorry for your loss."

Warmth swirled in my chest at his sweet condolences. He wasn't angry that I didn't tell him. He was the total opposite —understanding and kind. What was left of my walls were crumbling, and he grabbed my hand, turning me back to Hope's tree. *I should tell him everything.* A breeze blew through the woods as we stood and stared at the tree. Though silence was between us for a while, it was comfortable, and I felt as ease with him by my side. *Maybe later.* I knew I needed to tell him, but it just didn't feel right for the moment.

"Not a day goes by that I don't think about her, or the future I imagined we'd have together. It took a long time for me to be happy for other people when I heard they were pregnant. I couldn't understand why I had to lose her. God has helped me a lot, though. Hope will always have a piece of my heart with her in heaven." Taking a deep breath, I turned to him and said, "We can go now."

He nodded. Leading me by the hand, we walked out of the woods and over to the shoreline. Stopping in front of the dock, I stole a quick glance at Charlie's face and saw tears welling as he grimaced. We stood for a few moments in silence, and then Charlie cleared his throat. "We used to go fishing on Thursdays when I was a boy."

"Every week?" I asked, curious if that was the reason for the weekly visit to the diner.

Charlie smiled. "No. Not *every* Thursday, but we did go out to eat at Dixie's every Thursday for breakfast, regardless of whether we fished. It didn't matter how crazy life got. He'd always do it. Some days, especially when I got a little older, like High School, I *dreaded* going. But . . . he made me. A few times, we didn't exchange more than a couple of words, while other times, I was late getting to school because we talked the whole time. He gave me his time, whether I wanted it or not . . ." Charlie pulled out the pocket watch I saw him with that first day at the inn and became choked up again as he smoothed his thumb over an etched train that was on the cover of it. "He was a good dad and gave me his time freely. I've struggled so hard with the loss of him, Amy." He turned to me with tear-filled eyes. "Jody found a buyer for the boat. A guy from Coeur d'Alene is coming to look at it here in a few days or so." He put the pocket watch back into his pocket.

"You okay?" I asked, reaching out and grasping onto his hand.

He shrugged and looked out toward the water. "I don't really have an option, do I?"

Shaking my head slowly, I said, "I guess not."

He wiped the tears from his eyes and peered over his shoulder, back toward the path leading back up alongside the house. "I need to go punch the clock for a few hours on this project I'm working on at work."

"Okay," I replied. "What were you doing here?"

"I always come down to the lake to clear my head. The water brings my soul a peace and calmness I can't find anywhere else."

I smiled. "I understand that."

He stepped closer to me and pushed a loose strand of hair behind my ear as he smiled and looked into my eyes. He looked happy again. It was if all that pain over the loss of his father faded, if only for that brief moment in time. Leaning in, he kissed me gently. Warmth came rushing through my lips and took over my body, pushing out the worry, sadness, and hurt that had been plaguing me that morning. Though we both had heartaches, we were two souls, completely vulnerable to one another. What we had dampened the pains of life, and each other's company brought comfort to our souls and peace to our minds.

His hand framed my face as we continued to kiss, each moment better than the last. Kissing on my neck, his hands slid down my sides and to my hips. I brought my arms up around his neck as his lips worked their way further down my neckline. Charlie's affection for me reached into my soul and reinvigorated a part of me that I had lost. I dropped my head back, and his lips trailed up my neck and toward my face until I tipped my chin to him and his lips found mine.

Looking deep into his eyes as I pulled back from our kiss, I saw love. Waves of warmth continued to push through me, and I leaned in again, letting myself fall further into his existence.

STOPPING IN AT DIXIE'S DINER ON THE WAY BACK HOME TO pick up my check, I saw Diego and Miley chatting a bit more than usual. Curious, I went over to them. Diego was talking about barbecuing a bunch of food and inviting almost half the town over to his home. *That could be fun for Charlie and me,* I thought.

"What's up, guys?" I asked.

Diego tipped his chin. "Barbecue at my house tonight. My wife wants to see these pretty girls I'm working with." He laughed. "She thinks you two are a threat to her."

I let out a laugh. "She's that kind of gal, huh?"

He nodded slowly. "She's a sweet, sweet woman, but insecure to a fault. It will be a fine time. Burgers, hot dogs, that kind of thing."

"Sounds good. What time?" I asked.

"Seven."

"Bring your boyfriend," Miley added sarcastically.

I went flush. "Shut it, Miley," I scolded. Diego let out a laugh and turned to pull burgers from the grill. Miley grabbed my arm and pulled me away from the window to talk to me near the server station.

"Tell me how the date went with him." Her eyes were wide with excitement to hear the details.

I smiled. "It was *good.*"

"Good how? What happened? Don't be a brat. Details!" She leaned a hand on the server station.

"We kissed and things got . . . *Very* heated."

She shoved my shoulder back and said, "Shut up!" Smiling, Miley said, "So the shy and quiet girl sounds like she's finally coming out of her shell. Just took a year to hatch."

Her comment reminded me of last night's encounter with John. *I hope he really left town.* "There's more."

"I thought you were a church girl," Miley said.

Shooing my hand at her, I said, "No. Not Charlie." Leaning in, I got quiet. "My ex-husband is in town."

Her eyes bulged. "What? You were married?"

I nodded and took a deep breath. *I have to tell her.* My heart spilled out to Miley at the server station in Dixie's Diner. My story didn't leave any stone unturned, and by the end of it, we were both in tears.

"I'm so sorry you've had to hold that in all this time. You have to tell Charlie, Amy—I mean, Serenah." Miley placed her hands on both my shoulders and shook her head. "This is too big."

"I know. I'm going to tell him tonight after the barbecue."

"Good."

Leaning in, I gave Miley a hug. "I love you. You've been like the sister I never had."

CHAPTER 11

*A*rriving at the barbecue with a bag of chips in one hand and a twelve-pack of soda in the other, I saw Diego manning the barbecue as people crowded the back yard. *Guess this is a bigger barbecue than I anticipated.* Seeing me, he pointed me out to whom I suspected was his wife, Kathy. She waved and smiled as she came my direction.

"So you're *Amy,*" she said, grabbing the bag of chips.

"Yep. Kathy, I take it?"

She nodded. "We can put these inside," she said, leading me over to the house and up the back steps. Coming inside to the kitchen, I set the soda down on the table.

"How long have you and Diego been married?" I asked.

"Fifteen years this August."

Raising an eyebrow, I said, "Wow. That's awesome."

"Are you dating anyone?" she asked, leaning against the counter for support. Kathy didn't wait even a minute to go straight to the reason she threw together the barbecue. It was kind of strange but a tad bit funny that she would think Miley or I would be interested in Diego. He was a cute man, but he was older and married, two things that were deal breakers to any decent person. There was no way of knowing Kathy's reasons. Maybe they had issues in the past that I didn't know about.

"Dating? Um . . . yeah. No. I don't really know *what* it is right now. I invited him to the barbecue, though." Fumbling with my words, I felt embarrassed. Not knowing how to define what Charlie and I had made me feel uncomfortable. We had kissed already a few different times and shared parts of our life we didn't really share with just anyone. "I think we're together. It's still new."

Kathy smiled and went over to the fridge. Pulling out a container of Hawaiian punch and a bottle of lemon-lime soda, she brought them over to the table. "Those early parts of the relationship are so . . . electric, aren't they? It's not like the hum-drum of marriage at all."

"Yeah. I was married once. It's different, that's for sure."

She furrowed an eyebrow as she poured the punch into a clear bowl on the table. "Diego never mentioned you were married before."

My heart took a freefall from what felt like a cliff. I had forgotten the conversation Diego and I had about a month after my arrival to Newport. He had asked if I was ever married because of a tan line along my finger. I lied, claiming it was just a ring a boyfriend gave me. I was more protective back then of my past. Thinking quickly in the moment with Kathy, I found an excuse that would work in more ways than one. I said, "I don't tell Diego *everything,* Kathy. He's just the line cook where I work."

Her smile widened with my words. I was glad to ease her insecurities. Turning back to the sliding glass door, I about jumped when I saw John out in the backyard chatting Mayor Laney's ear up. *What's he doing here?* The mayor let out a hearty laugh and grabbed his belly. *Ugh, he's laying it on thick.* That was John, always rubbing elbows and making everyone around him fall in love with him. It came more natural to him than breathing did. No matter the occasion or the event, he'd have people eating out of the palm of his hand. My theory on it was that John hated himself so much that if he could convince a room full of people to love him, maybe that, in turn, would help him love himself.

"Amy?" Kathy said, breaking my concentration.

"What?" I asked, turning to her.

"I asked how the car was working for you."

I nodded. "Oh, it's great. I've had zero problems with it." Pointing out the sliding glass door, I continued, "I'm going to go mingle, I think."

"Could you help me with something first?" she asked, pointing to the counter. Looking over, I saw tomatoes and lettuce sitting on a cutting board. "I need that all sliced and chopped for the burgers."

Smiling, I reluctantly said, "Sure."

"Thanks," she replied and went into the living room. Heading over to the counter, I picked up the knife and began slicing a tomato. There was a window right in front of me, so every few cuts, I'd glance up and locate John out in the yard. *Why does he have to be here?* With John being at the barbecue, things could become tense and awkward as soon as Charlie arrived. The best I could do was make sure to get to Charlie before John did.

Slice.

The blade cut through my index finger, sending gobs of blood oozing out. "Ah!" I shouted, dropping the blade and hurrying a few paces over to the sink. Glancing over my shoulder, I called out to Kathy, "Could you get me a Band-Aid? I cut myself."

"Okay . . ." Her tone made me feel stupid. *It was an accident, lady,* I thought to myself.

Letting the water rush over the cut, I glanced over and

saw a spot of blood on the counter. *Should have paid better attention.* Kathy soon came in with a Band-Aid and helped me get it bandaged up and the counter cleaned. "Sorry about that," I said, returning back to the cutting board. Peering out the window, I couldn't see John.

Kathy shook her head and smiled at me as she came over. Taking the blade from my hand, she said, "It's okay. I'll take care of this. Run along outside and mingle."

Should have cut myself in the beginning, I thought. Leaving through the sliding glass door, I surveyed the yard and the roughly two dozen faces that were on the lawn. *Where did he go? Wait . . .* Pulling my cellphone from my pocket, I saw it was 7:45pm, fifteen minutes past when Charlie was supposed to be there. *No, no, no!* Hurrying toward the corner of the house, I was stopped by Emma.

"Where you off to in such a hurry?" she asked.

"I can't talk right now," I replied. Side-stepping her, I continued to the corner.

Pieces of my heart crumbled as I rounded the corner and saw Charlie walking away from a conversation with John. If Satan had a doppelgänger, I was convinced John was his. How could a man who claims to love me seek to destroy everything I care about? How could one person be so sadistic?

"What did you say to him?" My words were sharp as I approached John and shoved him backward. There was no threat of him retaliating. There were too many witnesses.

He laughed. "Just told him who you *actually* were. Like your real name, for starters. You've been living a lie with these people."

"How did you even know who he was?"

John broke out in song. *"Every step you take, every move you make, I'll be watching you!"* He stopped singing and shook his head. "I saw your little passion fest down at Riverfront Park with him the other day."

Pushing past John, I ran down the driveway and out to the front to see Charlie crossing the street over to his car. "Charlie!" I called out.

He turned back to me for a moment and then opened his car door.

Sprinting, I kicked gravel up in the driveway as I made my way out to the road. *"Please."*

He stopped and looked back at me like he didn't even know who I was. His eyes glistened, and the hurt I saw stung. Coming across the road the rest of the way, I arrived over to him. When I reached for his hand, he pulled it away. "Don't, Amy. Well, I mean . . . *Serenah?*"

"I was going to tell you." Tears welled in my eyes as I felt every part of my life shatter into little shards of glass.

He let out a sarcastic laugh. "When did you *plan* on telling me that you're married and have a husband?"

"Tonight. You don't understand. John is a *bad* man, Charlie."

"You're right. I don't understand. You had a baby, a husband and a whole other life. I don't know you. I didn't even know your real name."

"You might have known me by a different name and nothing of my past, but what we had was real. The way we feel about each other—"

"The way I *felt* about you was based on concrete information." He peered back toward Diego's house and continued, "I don't want to come between a husband and wife. That isn't right." He went to get into his car, but I grabbed his arm.

"Why do you think I ran across the country and changed my name, Charlie? You think I just didn't like the guy? It wasn't that simple."

He looked at me and shrugged. "Telling the truth is always simple."

"I never *lied.*"

Charlie got in his car and shut the door. Turning the key over, he rolled the window down and said, "Goodbye, whoever you are."

The taillights of his car blurred in my vision as tears rolled from my eyes and onto my cheeks. My heart was breaking. The twisted, mangled mess of emotion all stemmed from one source—John. I felt as if he would follow me to the ends of the earth, making sure I'd never be happy and always destroying any good that would come into my life.

"Serenah, doll," John called out to me from the edge of the driveway of Diego's house. "Why don't you come back over here and let me introduce you to the Mayor? He's going to let me head the reconstruction project on City Hall." John's voice in that moment set me ablaze. It was like hot coals being raked over my open wounds. Turning to face him as he stood on the other side of the street, I saw a few of the locals around him, but I didn't care—I charged him.

I laid a punch into his face for everything he had done. The marriage, the beatings, the stress that led me to miscarry, and now, Charlie. He didn't dodge my attack. Instead, he let me hit him and send him crashing to the driveway, spilling the drink in his hand. Frank and Sue were a few paces back and saw it. They shook their heads in disappointment at me. They didn't understand. The locals who stood by his side were Jackie and Monty, who ran the convenience store on Main Street. Monty helped John to his feet, and Jackie stepped between me and John as I panted heavily, trying to catch my breath.

"You can't hit people because you don't like them. Didn't your mother teach you any manners?" Jackie asked. She looked mad. So did Monty. I was the bad guy in all their minds.

Monty let go of John's arm and added, "Obviously, she was taught it was okay to lie too. Right, *Serenah?*"

Diego approached with a somber expression on his face. "I think it's best you go."

Nodding my head, I agreed. Not because I was misbehaving, but because John had already managed to get everybody on his side. Turning around, I headed to my car to leave. *Unbelievable.* As I felt eyes on my back, my blood boiled inside. As I drove, I began crying out to the Lord to help me, save me and make me whole again. I needed a miracle, now more than ever, if I was going to survive.

CHAPTER 12

*A*voiding Jody's phone calls, knowing John was most likely staying there, I kept a low profile for weeks following the barbecue. The Monday after the barbecue, I turned in a petition for divorce against John. There wasn't a point in putting it off now, since John knew where I lived and an address wouldn't give me away anymore. The damage done at the barbecue echoed through my entire life. Charlie vanished and wasn't coming into the diner anymore, and Emma stopped coming in too. I had tried to get ahold of her a few times, but her home phone always went to voicemail. Diego kept to himself in the back, only exchanging dialogue when it was vital for the job. Even Frank and Sue didn't want to chat anymore when they came in for their meatloaf and potatoes. He was turning everybody in town against me, and I was left feeling alone and isolated. Joe even kept his distance and conversation to a minimum when he finally came back to fix my roof last week. Miley was the only one who was there for me, but she had left to Texas to see her sickly father, so it was only phone calls here and there that got me through the weeks.

I'd see John randomly around town, sweet talking the locals, but I made sure to avoid him at all costs. I even abandoned a bag of groceries one day to avoid him. He was busy with the town I cared about. My biggest regret was how easy I'd made it for him. With my fake name and phony story, he was able to convince everybody I was just a washed-up loser who ran away from him. He painted a story for the whole town about how I only ran away because I didn't like him and how he found me to bring me back home. He claimed love was what brought him here to Newport, and love would take me back with him. John had them right where he wanted them. Before she had left to Texas, Miley told me that John told her that he'd be willing to stay in Newport if that meant being with me. When she asked me about why he would do this, I simply replied, 'Because he can. He has the time and money to do whatever he feels like.'

It had been three weeks since the barbecue, and I was working a morning shift on a Wednesday at Dixie's when the policeman, Brody Jenkins, the guy Miley had dated a few months back, walked into the diner. He surveyed the restaurant and then came to me once he spotted me near the computer.

"These are for you, Serenah," he said, emotionless in his tone.

"He got to you too?" I asked, taking the papers from him.

"John's a good guy. Everybody thinks you should give him a chance."

I laughed as I shook my head. "You don't even know him, Brody." My eyes looked down to see the court papers for the divorce from John. My eyes welled with tears of joy as I saw it was finally coming to fruition. Ninety from that moment, I'd be divorced from John, and that chapter of my life would be officially over. Wiping my eyes, I put the papers in my purse below the computer. "Thanks for bringing them by."

He forced a half-smile and said, "You're welcome. Think about John, *please.*" He took his leave and I returned to waiting tables.

ENJOYING A GLASS OF WINE AS I CELEBRATED VICTORY WITH MY only friend around—Milo—I sat out on the porch in my rocking chair. With the papers and glass of wine on the table beside me, I rocked gently in the chair as I petted Milo. "No more Mrs. Wollocks. Isn't that great?" I asked Milo as I glanced down at him.

He only continued to purr.

"It's good. Even though John's ruined everything I've been working toward. It's a good thing the divorce is done." Scooting Milo off my lap, I stood up, picked up my glass of wine, and walked over to the railing. It was unpainted but sturdy. I leaned against it and looked up to the stars. Praying, I asked God to bring me wisdom about whether I should just pack everything up and move away from Newport. Closing my eyes, I outstretched my arms over the railing and dropped my head in the gap between them and said, "Oh, God. *Help me.*

"Decided on going back to God after you left me?" John said from the far end of the porch.

Jerking my head up, I cocked it his way and glared. "You aren't welcome here."

Rolling his eyes, he climbed up onto the porch and walked up beside me. Leaning his arms onto the railing, he continued as he looked out to the evening skies. "Had an interesting chat today with Brody. He uh . . . brought me some papers."

I nodded. "Yeah. Maybe you didn't realize it when I left and tried to vanish without a trace, but I don't want to be with you, John."

His jaw clenched as he stood up and turned toward me.

I sensed the anger and turned away, heading quickly into my house. He followed. Pulling open the entry table door drawer, I couldn't find the pepper spray I had put there.

"You think I'm stupid? I got rid of your dumb spray." He glanced up at the ceiling. "Looks like you got your roof repaired. By the way . . . how many men do you have wrapped around your finger?"

"I don't," I said curtly as I thought about the bat in the coat closet nearby. Dashing across the floor to the closet, I yanked open the door.

"Yeah, took that too." He went over to the couch and sat down, crossing a leg over his other one. "Look, honey. I quit drinking, and I'm here to win you back." He laughed. "You want to live in this dirty little town with your little friends? That's fine. We can sell our house in Albany. I'm already moved into a month-to-month apartment over on Shirley Avenue, by the hospital."

"It's not that easy, *John.*"

"Why?" he asked, shaking his head as he uncrossed his legs and leaned forward with his hands out. Without a response from me, he stood up and approached me. Backing my steps up, I pressed up against the wall as he got inches from my face. Tilting his head, he asked, "Why's it not that *easy?* The drinking was the problem, and it's gone."

"It wasn't just the drinking, *John.* It was the fact that you hit me." My eyes peered into the kitchen as I thought about dashing into there to grab a knife.

"I did it while drunk. I don't drink anymore. Problem solved." He shrugged.

Ducking, I turned and headed into the kitchen. He

gripped my wrist with a hand, and I shook it off. "You hit me when you were sober too. Right before I left."

He squinted and looked to ponder for a moment. I continued to head into the kitchen, but he grabbed my shoulder and yanked me back and up against the wall. He clutched my throat with his hand and pushed me against the wall, causing a picture frame to fall. "You're not going to tell me how things are going to happen. This is my world! My rules!"

"Hit me, John. It's what you were *always* best at."

He did.

The first punch landed directly into my jaw, the next one my eye. Falling to the ground, I curled up and began to cry as he kicked my ribs. "You forced me to do this! You could have had me back with ease, you stupid, stupid woman." He stopped after a few more kicks, cleared his throat, and adjusted his tie. Turning, he walked out of my house as Milo walked in from the porch. My heart raced as I curled tighter into a ball on the floor. Crying out to the Lord, I prayed he'd help me in my time of need.

"Please, Lord, take this pain from me. *Help* me figure out what to do." Closing my eyes, I felt Milo's fur press up against my arm that was wrapped over my head. My pulse began to slow, and a comfort came to me that I could not describe if I tried. It wasn't from a feline. No, the comfort was divine. Continuing to pray, I asked God for His will to be done and clarity to come to me. My life was not my own. I needed help.

After a few moments, I crawled over to the coffee table and grabbed my phone. Calling Brody, I tried telling him what had happened and he didn't believe me. I hung up. John had everyone brainwashed, and I felt more hopeless than I had ever felt in my life. I needed God more than ever if I was going to survive.

CHAPTER 13

With trembling hands, I did my best to put makeup on the next morning. Frustration rose in me as I couldn't cover the bruised eye. Finally giving up, I threw my foundation against the bathroom wall, shattering the bottle into pieces. Glaring into the mirror, I shook my head as tears welled in my eyes. Clutching the bathroom sink on both sides, I prayed, asking God why I had to go through this again. My own will told me to pack everything up and run, but that still quiet voice inside me told me to trust God. My nerves settled moments after my prayer, and I relaxed my shoulders as I stood looking at my battered face. "Nobody's going to believe John did this to me."

There was still another hour before I needed to be at work that morning, so I decided to go out to the *Inn at the Lake* since I now knew John had moved out. The still waters helped calm the raging storm that I felt inside. Walking the dock to the end, I sat down. Though I had prayed more times than I could count in the last twelve hours, I bowed my head and went to the Lord again. My heart was broken, and I felt trapped and alone in a world of isolation.

Hearing the sound of footsteps hit the dock, I jumped. Jerking my head around, I saw it was Emma—I breathed a sigh of relief. She was in a robe again. Turning my eyes back to the water, I said as she approached behind me, "Hey, stranger."

She coughed and continued up to my side. "Help me down," she said. Reaching my left hand up, I helped her to a seat beside me without turning my head. Breathing a relieving sigh as she sat, she said, "I'm sorry I haven't been around lately . . . I've been sick."

Turning my head to her without thinking about the bruise, I said, "I'm sorry."

Emma caught a glimpse of my wounded face, and her eyes went wide. "What did he do?"

Tears immediately started pouring from my eyes as I felt my heart spill open. She pulled me into her chest and combed her fingers through my hair. Her touch was comforting, and it reminded me of when I was a little girl and my mother would hold me after I got hurt. I cried harder. "He won't leave me alone, Emma. I don't know what to do anymore."

"How did he get to you?" she asked, gently releasing me from her chest to look at me.

"He just showed up at my house. I was out on my porch."

"You have protection?" Emma asked.

"I had mace, but he took it."

Emma nodded as her eyes traced my bruised face. "You call the police?"

"Brody's on his side. Everyone loves him."

Frowning, Emma shook her head. "He's a smooth talker. I met him when he was staying at the inn a few nights. He had Jody and Wayne laughing up a storm. I hadn't ever heard Wayne laugh the way I did that night. He can talk, that's for sure."

I nodded. "It's his specialty, unfortunately."

"Carry protection on you and get a security system. That's what you'll have to do," Emma said. Coughing again, she grabbed onto my shoulder as the coughing fit lasted a few moments. Once it was over, she said, "I want you to know first—I'm selling the inn at the end of the summer."

"Why?" I asked, sitting up straighter and launching myself out of thoughts of John. "It's been in your family for generations."

"Jody's moving to Arizona. Wayne's health has declined over the last six months, and the climate is better down there. I'd run it, but I'm too old." A frown set deep into her face as she looked out to the water.

I asked, "Why don't you find someone to run it?"

She looked over at me, made a point to look at the bruise on my jaw, and then said, "I would, but the only person I have in mind is probably about to flee town."

Furrowing my eyebrows, I shook my head. "Me?"

"You," Emma said. "I've known about Jody and Wayne leaving for a while now. My eyes have been peeled, watching for someone with a good heart and the perfect soul to run it. You're the one."

Glancing over my shoulder at the massive bed and breakfast behind us up beyond the paths that ran through the flower bed, I gulped. "Managing and operating a place of this caliber is something I could never dream of doing. My skills and abilities are lacking."

Emma laughed. "I'm sure you'd be fine with the proper training. My offer's on the table, Serenah. It will stay there for the next week, and then I'll be approaching a real estate agent."

"I—" I began to say, but Emma interrupted.

"*Pray* about it."

ARRIVING AT THE DINER THAT MORNING I CLOCKED IN AND began to put on my apron. Seeing there were five minutes before 9:13, I tried to remind myself that Charlie wasn't coming in, just like he hadn't for several weeks now. Though I drilled that fact into my brain, it didn't quench the hope that resided in my heart. Sure enough, at 9:13, I looked over at the door and paused. *Please . . .*

The clock struck 9:14 and the moment passed.

It was that way every Thursday since the barbecue happened. My hope for his sudden reappearance drove me nuts, but I knew it'd never go away.

Later that morning, around 10:30, the front door of Dixie's diner opened and in walked Charlie. Turning my bruised face away from the door as I stood at the server station, I froze in place. When I saw him approaching out of the corner of my eye, my heart began pounding so hard that I thought it was going to leap from my chest.

"Serenah?" he said in a smooth, soft voice as I still stood frozen, not turning to him.

"Charlie . . ."

"I need to say something to you. Without you interrupting me."

"Okay."

"I don't really understand what went on with you and John, and honestly, I don't care. After the barbecue, I left town. I headed up to a lake in Idaho where my dad and I used to fish when I was a kid. I fished, camped and did a lot of praying. The point is, I had to do some soul searching. There was some stuff I was holding onto from the past that I needed to let go of. I came to realize that what you said was true. I didn't fall in love with your past or your name, but your soul."

Tears streamed from my eyes as his words wrapped themselves around my heart and sent waves of warmth crashing through my body.

"I don't care about John or anything in your past. I don't even care if you killed someone. Wait. Okay, if you killed someone, that would be bad. But what I am saying is I want you, Serenah. The *real* you. I don't want any more lies or secrets." He touched my shoulder and pulled me to face him.

Letting him turn me was the hardest thing I could do. I knew he'd see the bruises, and I knew how much it would hurt him. As I turned, I felt my tears quicken down my cheeks. When his eyes fell onto my face, anger fired through him like a shotgun going off.

"No!" he shouted. Turning around immediately, he rushed to the front door before I could stop him. Chasing after him, I came outside and saw him cross two streets over to City Hall and deck John in the face. My heart catapulted into my throat as I saw John hit the grass in front of City Hall. Charlie stood over him like my gallant knight.

My cheeks flooded with tears as I saw the other men that were with John wrestle Charlie to the ground and lay a few punches into his face. "No!" I shouted. Turning back to the diner, I saw Wendy at the door waving me back inside. Glancing toward the scene again, I saw Brody cuffing Charlie. *He only reacted to the evidence that was written on my face . . .* My heart yearned to be there for Charlie in that moment. Watching as Brody led him over to the police cruiser, I told myself I'd go down to the station after work.

AFTER MY SHIFT, I HEADED DOWN TO THE LOCAL JAIL. BRODY was there and agreed to talk to me, but not until he finished up the report. Waiting out in the lobby, I nervously tapped my fingers on the plastic armrest of the chair. *I can't believe Charlie did that. That's twice now that he's been violent. Should I worry?* Not sure what to think of the situation, I just focused on swaying Brody about John and about Charlie. The hour wait in that lobby felt like an eternity, but then he finally called me back.

"Serenah," Brody said with a wave of his hand and a frown on his face. He led me through a white cement hallway and down to a metal door that led into his office. Taking a seat in the chair across from the desk, I scooted closer as he went around and sat.

"Thanks for talking to me," I said. "Charlie's a really good guy, and—" I began to say, but he interrupted me by raising his hand.

"Charlie's a fine guy." Brody's eyes caught my bruise. "What happened to your face?"

I leaned in and said, "Remember? I told you John hit me! John was upset about the divorce papers and attacked me at my house."

He squinted as he looked me over as if I were lying.

"I'm not lying, Brody. You think I inflicted these wounds onto myself? C'mon, you *know* me."

He laughed. "I thought I did."

"You do, though." I adjusted in my seat. "I ran away from John because he was abusive and cruel to me. I had to go by a different name because he has so much money, I figured he'd track me down. And see? He did anyway. It didn't matter that I used a different name. He found me anyway." Seeing him not fully convinced, I said, "You've probably known Charlie for a long time."

"I have," he agreed with a nod. "Our moms did a Bible study for years when we were younger."

"Okay. So is violence something that's typical of him? Ever?"

"No, but that doesn't matter. He broke the law, Serenah. There's nothing I can do about that. I have to do my job."

"You could help his case though. You were the arresting officer."

He nodded, but he still seemed uneasy about the conversation.

"I have a plan, Brody. I can get John to screw up, and we can get him out of this town. You just have to believe me." Though I didn't have a plan, I knew it sounded better if I did.

He looked at my black eye again and said, "If what you say is true about him hitting you, I don't want him in my town." He looked at the door and said, "I'll release Charlie, but you'd better make sure he isn't back in my custody."

Smiling, I jumped up and launched myself across the desk, hugging him. "Thank you."

Brody said, "Thank me by not making me look stupid."

$\mathcal{I}$t took another hour for Brody to release him from jail, but he got it done. Charlie came walking out with his head dipped and hands dug into each of his jean pockets. He seemed upset. We walked out to my car, and we didn't speak a word. The street lights outside played through the windshield of the car. As we drove through town, I saw his bloodied knuckles sitting on his lap. He really did a number on John's face too. A few of the guys who were at City Hall took him to the hospital as Brody hauled Charlie off to jail. It looked like something out of a movie, not anything I had ever seen in real life.

Charlie broke the silence by clearing his throat and saying, "I know you've seen me hit two people now, but I promise, it's not how I usually handle problems."

"You do speak," I replied, glancing over at him. "I know, Charlie. You were triggered when you saw what he did to me. I hate to romanticize violence, but it was truly *heroic*. Not because you clobbered the guy, but because you defended me. You're a good man with a good soul, and I know that."

T.K. CHAPIN

He smiled at me and reached his bloodied hand over the armrest and grasped onto mine. His touch felt secure and warm. We held hands the rest of the drive to his car that was parked in front of Dixie's Diner.

When the wheels of my car stopped, he turned to me and undid his seatbelt. Before he had a chance to do anything, I undid my seatbelt and leaned across the armrest and into his arms. He brought his hands up to the sides of my face and gently pulled me in, kissing me passionately. Charlie's touch was more intoxicating than ever. I wanted him to never leave me again. I forgot the world and all the problems that came along with it and just wanted to live in that moment forever. Our passion continued as our breaths grew heavier and our skin hotter. Each touch of his lips on my skin drove me crazier. As he ran his lips along my neck, warmth tickled my chest and traveled down my body.

Then he stopped.

Charlie gave me a look like he wanted every part of me and said, "Another kiss of your lips might kill me."

I smiled as he was about to get out and asked, "Could you come over? Stay with me?"

He raised a suspicious eyebrow. "Umm . . ."

"Not like that. I'm just . . . scared right now."

Nodding, he said, "Yeah, I'll come over. Let me drive my car there."

"Okay."

He leaned over the armrest and gently cupped my face, making sure to avoid the bruises. Softly, he kissed my lips and said, "Guess I didn't die." He smiled as he continued, "See you in a few."

WHEN I ARRIVED HOME, I STAYED OUT ON THE PORCH WAITING

for Charlie to show up. I made sure to be holding a knife just in case John decided to show up too. After a few minutes went by, I figured Charlie must have run out of gas or something and needed to stop. After an hour went by, I became worried. He wasn't picking up his cellphone when I tried to call. Becoming frustrated, I went out to my car and got in. My cellphone rang—it was Jody. Since it was after ten o'clock, I didn't know what to expect.

"Serenah. I need you to get in your car and come up to the hospital."

"What happened?"

"Charlie has been in an accident. He said he couldn't stop when he came to a red light, and he barreled right through it when a truck coming through the intersection hit him." Jody's voice was under complete control and poise as she spoke. My heart, on the other hand, had zero control. Tears streamed down my cheeks as my throat clenched.

"It was John Wollocks," I said with absolute confidence.

"What?" Jody asked.

"John Wollocks cut the brake lines in his car."

"No, he didn't," Jody replied. "John's been at the hospital all day."

"Whatever. I'll be there in a minute," I said curtly. Hanging up my phone, I threw it into my passenger seat and peeled out of my driveway. I knew it was John. Praying as I drove, I asked for God's wisdom. *Why? Why does this have to happen to me, God? To Charlie?* It was one thing to put myself in danger when it came to John, but it was entirely another thing to put someone else in the midst of it. I already lost my daughter because of John. I refused to lose Charlie too.

WHEN I WALKED INTO THE ER, I EXPECTED TO FIND CHARLIE

in a bed with machines hooked up to him, but he wasn't. He was sitting on the edge of a hospital bed laughing with a doctor about forgetting a semicolon in a line of computer code and spending hours attempting to diagnose the problem—computer talk I didn't understand. His arm was in a sling, but everything else looked like minor scrapes and bruises.

"Wow," I said, walking in and setting my purse on the chair that sat against the wall. The doctor placed papers on the bed beside Charlie and excused himself from the room. As he rounded the corner out the doorway, I continued, "I thought you were messed up from the wreck."

He shrugged. "Just a broken arm. I told Jody to tell you to come up here, but make sure you weren't alarmed."

"It's always hard to know how serious something is with her. She is monotone most of the time."

He nodded. "That is true." Glancing at the doorway for a moment, he paused and then looked back at me as he lowered his voice. "Think John did this?"

"I can't see who else would," I replied.

Rubbing the stubble of his jaw line, he smiled at me. "You'd better be worth all this trouble, Serenah."

Smirking, I shrugged.

"Come here," he said. I stepped over to him, and he pulled me in for a kiss with his good arm. "I know you are worth every bit of it. We've just got to get him out of Newport."

I smiled. "I'm glad you're okay, Charlie. I have no idea short of running how to get him out of our lives. Look what I went through to leave him the first time, and he still found me."

Charlie's eyes looked up to the ceiling as he appeared to be thinking. "Is it all women or just you that he abuses?"

"What do you mean?" I asked.

"If we set him up with someone, would he like . . . hit her by the end of the night?"

I laughed but covered my mouth with a hand as I saw it was inappropriate. "Sorry. No. No woman is that stupid to *choose* to be with an abuser from the get go. It's not something that is just normally there from the beginning. Sorry."

He shrugged and shook his head. "No need to say sorry. I don't know anything about this kind of stuff. Just thinking. Hey, what if we can stage a thing with you?"

Raising an eyebrow, I said, "Continue."

"Like a video camera or me and Brody hiding out while he beats you up."

Shaking my head, I said, "How would you even predict that? It's not like he just comes around and beats me every day at a certain time."

"Dang."

Touching his shoulder, I said, "It's okay. We'll figure something out."

"I got it. What if we agitate him *really* bad? He's got to have a short-tempered fuse somewhere in all that fake facade he has going on."

"That could work."

"There's a community potluck at the *Inn at the Lake* tomorrow. I'm sure he'll be going." Charlie slid off the hospital bed and onto his feet. Turning to his hospital bed, he scooped the papers up and set them between his sling and chest. "Look at that. It's a paper holder." He smiled as he seemed entertained with the slightest thing. Though he had almost been killed by my ex-husband, he seemed goofy and light-hearted in the moment, and I appreciated that. It took away a lot of the guilt I had been feeling.

"We'll get him at the potluck," I said. "Lots of kissing and touching between us. That kind of thing would make him go nuts."

Charlie raised an eyebrow and came closer to me, pulling me in close to his chest. Smiling, he said, "We should practice." Leaning in, he kissed me and then smiled again as he pulled back. "I could do this all day."

Smiling, I lifted my hands to his face and framed his jaw with my hands as I kissed him passionately. Charlie's arms, or rather *arm* for now, was exactly where I wanted to be. He was everything that I wanted in a man, and though it took a broken road to find him, I'd do it all again if it meant being with him. We left the hospital and headed back to my house.

When we arrived home, he got out first and scouted out the perimeter with the knife in hand that I left on the railing of the porch. After he finished, he came back to the car and gave me a nod. Getting out, I said, "Thank you."

"I'm your protector," he stated. "I might only have one good arm now, but that won't stop me from kicking the snot out of him again."

I touched his shoulder and said, "You can't do that unless we have some sort of evidence against him."

"If he's here, that's evidence enough."

We went inside, and I made Charlie a big dinner even though it was after midnight. Chicken, mashed potatoes and corn. After we finished eating, he set his napkin down on his plate and smiled across the table as our eyes met. "This right here. This is what life's about."

"Food?" I asked as I finished chewing a bite of chicken.

He shook his head and held out his hands. "Spending time with people you care about. A home cooked meal is nice, don't get me wrong. But just . . . just sitting here with you makes me so happy, Serenah."

"I agree." Standing up, I took both of our plates into the kitchen and set them in the sink. "What's the deal with your job? They going to let you come back?"

Sighing, he replied, "No. They weren't going to let me leave, so I just quit."

My eyebrows went up and I looked over at him. "What about money? Bills?"

"I never liked paying bills anyway." He laughed. "I'm just kidding. I already set everything up for that side business a few days before I quit. There are a couple of projects I already have lined up from old customers that don't do business with Ikan anymore."

"Wow," I said, coming back over to the table. Resting a hand on the back of my chair, I nodded. "So you're finally going to do it."

"Yep." Standing up, he pushed in his chair and walked around the table to me. My heart fluttered as his fingers touched my arm and made their way up my shoulder and to my neck. Tilting his head, he said, "I'll have all the time in the world to spend with you. That is, if you can stand me."

The words warmed my soul. There were no limits to the amount of time I wanted to spend with Charlie. "You seem so different since you've come back."

He nodded. "I am. Once I realized that God didn't punish me by making me go through what I've been though, I've been a changed man."

"Why did He make you go through it?"

His fingers traced my neckline, back down my shoulder, and to my arm as he continued speaking. "Going through difficulties is part of life. It's how you come out the other end that really matters. God showed me that I can help others who are struggling by my own experience. God willing, I'll be a certified Christian counselor at 'A New Me in Christ' in a couple of years. Just as a side passion project of sorts. That's my hope." Taking his hand, Charlie placed it on my shoulder and said, "May I have this dance, my dear?"

Smiling, I said with a dip of my knees, "you may." Laying

my head on his chest, we began to sway slowly in the dining room of my house. My thoughts turned inward as I began thinking about the abuse I endured. *Maybe my experience could help someone someday.* Charlie was a man who had crossed over from the dark shadows of sadness, possibly even depression, and come out a new man. He was an inspiration to push on through the dark times that I had found myself in. Tomorrow's community potluck could go well and according to plan or absolutely disastrous, but I had to trust God that He was in control.

CHAPTER 15

*A*rriving at the *Inn at the Lake* with my arm wrapped around Charlie's free arm, we went inside and were greeted by Jody in the kitchen. He stayed and chatted with her while I broke off into the dining area just outside the kitchen to sit down with Emma. She was reading a book while sitting at one of the tables near the French doors that led out to the balcony. Meanwhile, people were chatting in the living room beside the dining area and out on the balcony.

A summer breeze was blowing lightly through the dining area as I sat down in a chair across from her. Setting her book down, she greeted me with a warm smile and grasped my hand. "How are you, Serenah? That eye feeling any better?"

"I'll survive." My eyes peered over at Charlie to steal a glance at his laugh.

Emma caught it and commented, "You're in love."

Dismissing it, I furrowed my eyebrows and said, "No. Maybe someday, we'll be in love, but I don't think I'm there yet."

"Why?" she pressed.

"It takes a lot of time to fall in love."

Emma rocked her head back and forth a couple times. "Maybe a deeper love, but I believe true love has a blossoming moment."

John walked into the room out of nowhere and conjured all my anger inside with five words. "Ms. Montgomery and my wife."

Charlie overheard and came over from the kitchen. Leaning over my shoulder, he planted a kiss on my cheek and looked up at John, saying, "Ex-wife. *Right?*"

John's jaw clenched and he didn't respond.

Standing upright, Charlie said, "I see you have some lovely stitches from our little altercation yesterday. It's too bad you don't actually fight men, only women who can't fight back. I would have loved to see what you can do." Charlie told me what he was going to say to egg John on, and it was working flawlessly. John not only had a few stitches across an eyebrow, but a pretty swollen lip to top it off. John was already boiling and wanting to hit someone, judging by his clenched fist hanging by his side. He knew his reputation would be ruined if he caused a scene though.

Through his teeth, John said, "We're not divorced, *yet.*" He excused himself from the room and went into the living room to talk to the people there. I breathed a sigh of relief as he left, and Charlie sat down at the table with Emma and me. He looked at Emma with a smile and asked, "How are you doing?"

She beamed warmly. "Great. How's Ikan?"

Shaking his head as he looked down at the wine glasses and grapes on the placemat, he said, "I don't work there anymore. I'm starting my own business online."

"The internet?" Emma asked, perplexed. "I thought that

thing was only good for the Facebook and recipes. Huh. That's neat though, Charlie. As long as it's paying the bills."

He entertained her with a friendly smile and said, "You know what? I call it fakebook. There's just nothing that beats real face-to-face sit downs with someone like this, huh?"

"Yes," Emma said with a gleeful tone and smile. "I was just trying to tell Jody that the other day, and she went on and on about how wonderful social media is because the face-to-face conversations aren't available." She leaned in toward Charlie as she continued, "They're only unavailable when we don't make them a priority!"

It was cute to see Charlie engage so willingly with Emma. He listened to every word she said as we sat there for the next thirty minutes. He listened, smiled and nodded as Emma went on and on about how different America was since she was a child. Every moment that I witnessed him interact more with people that day sent me falling harder and harder for him. *Maybe Emma was right. Maybe I am in love.*

AFTER FILLING UP ON AN ASSORTMENT OF VARIOUS FINGER foods later in the day, I went out to the balcony to look at the water. It was beautiful, but a soft meow caught my attention from down below. Looking, I saw a neighborhood cat get a paw stuck between the dock and the grass. Setting my glass of water down on the railing, I journeyed to the far end of the deck and took the steps down to the path that led through the flower beds. Getting down to the cat near the water, I bent a knee and helped wiggle the cat's leg free. With a slight limp, the cat began to walk away, continuing into the nearby woods.

"I tried with you, Serenah," John said from behind me, causing me to jump. His voice was deep and steady.

T.K. CHAPIN

"John, what are you doing?" I asked, glancing up at the empty balcony.

Paranoid that someone could be watching, he jerked his head back behind to see if anyone was there.

Smelling liquor, I asked, "Have you been drinking?"

He shrugged and said, "So what if I have?"

Seeing a couple people walk out to the balcony in my peripheral vision, I antagonized him. "You're pathetic."

He grimaced. "You want to see pathetic? Try your little boy toy *Charlie*. I've seen you guys make out and play around like you two are a couple of teenagers." John laughed. "That's not a relationship."

"You cut his brake lines, didn't you?" I asked. Hope dwindled that the guests on the balcony could actually hear anything. They walked away from the railing. *They couldn't have heard anything . . .*

"You bet I did. Paid a guy to take care of it for me, but obviously, he didn't finish the job. Charlie needs to go away —he's a waste of space, but so is everything in the entire square mileage of this pathetic town."

Charlie appeared at the railing and shouted down from the top balcony, "You're not going to get away with this, John!"

"Really? What are you going to do?" He laughed. "It's not what you know. It's what you can prove. My alibi is airtight."

Jody appeared next to Charlie at the railing and said, "John. You need to leave now."

John furrowed his eyebrows and looked at me. *It worked. He was riled up for sure.* Begrudgingly, he climbed the path that led up around the house to the driveway out front. Charlie made sure to say something to Jody when John was in earshot about hanging out tonight to shoot pool with a buddy.

The trap was laid.

Charlie hurried down the path, pushing John on his way, down to the water. Wrapping his arm around me, he asked if I was okay. After assuring him I was fine, he told me about how he had spoken to Brody, and Brody wanted to be there to arrest John on sight of an altercation. The work John had lain with the town was beginning to crumble, and I knew he'd be furious. Though I didn't know what the night would bring, I did know one thing.

God was with me.

CHAPTER 16

*S*itting quietly, pretending to watch TV as I pet Milo, my heart raced with anticipation of John's arrival to my house that night. *How long would it take for him to come over?* Brody, Charlie and I took all the needed precautions going into the night. First—no cars. I drove them both over to my house. Second was safety. Charlie and Brody would only be a scream away, outside the kitchen window.

After a couple of hours passed and the clock struck eleven, my heart rate had lowered and I began nodding off. Being up half the previous night talking to Charlie was all fine and dandy when it happened, but I was paying the price now. Straining to keep my eyes open and on the TV show, I was jolted a bit awake by my phone buzzing—it was Charlie.

Charlie: Do you still think he's coming tonight?

Me: I don't know. It's getting late though.

Charlie: Brody's nodding off, but I'm going to stay awake and keep an eye out.

Me: Okay. Thanks.

. . .

GETTING UP, I WENT DOWN THE HALLWAY AND INTO THE bathroom. When I came back out into the living room, a gloved hand shot out from the corner and covered my mouth. A knife pressed against my throat. "Shut your pretty mouth and don't scream," he whispered.

Pushing me into the hallway, he forced me down to the bedroom. Screaming as loud as I could did nothing against the muffling fabrics of the glove. The sharp edge of the blade slid down the skin of my neck, causing small nicks. Tears poured from my eyes as hopelessness swallowed me whole. Keeping his hand over my mouth in the bedroom, he threw the blade onto the bed and pulled out a roll of duct tape from his coat pocket. My eyes widened as he used his teeth to pull a piece that'd fit over my lips. My screams again fell silent against his glove. Slapping the sticky silencer across my lips, he proceeded to add more layers and then taped my hands behind my back, binding me to my doom.

"You stupid woman," he said, pushing me down onto the bed. Jumping onto the bed, he stood over me and pulled me up to the pillows, positioning my head on one. Then he dropped down beside me and laid his head on the same pillow my head was against. Putting his hands behind his head, he looked at the ceiling took a deep breath. "I *never* wanted this kind of life for us, Serenah." He looked over at me. "It wasn't supposed to be like *this*. I never wanted to kill you."

Kill me? With those words echoing through my skull, I jerked my body and launched myself off the bed. He climbed over to the edge and grabbed my hair, pulling me up off the ground a few inches. My eyes watered heavily. Pushing through the pain, I yanked my head away, losing a great deal of hair in the process. Wiggling farther away, I was able to get up on my knees by using the night stand as an anchor point for my shoulder, and I turned to run. He lunged from the bed and grabbed onto my backside causing me to fall face first halfway to the door. Tears streamed down my cheeks and onto the duct tape as he pulled me by the legs back into the bedroom.

Please, Lord. Deliver me. Please!

Flipping me over onto my back, John's eyes seemed almost black as the night as he climbed on top of me. The man I had I fallen in love with what felt like a lifetime ago didn't exist anymore behind those eyes. He reached over to the bed and grabbed the dagger. Lifting it up into the air above his head, he said, "If I can't have you, nobody can."

Squeezing my eyes shut, I waited.

The stab didn't come, but instead came the sound of John toppling over. Opening my eyes, I saw Charlie on top of John, pinning him with his one good hand while his bad arm was pressed against his chest. Brody dashed in moments later through the doorway of the bedroom and helped subdue John. Cuffing him, Brody led John out of the room.

Charlie was in tears as he undid the duct tape from my head. "I'm so sorry I didn't hear him enter the house, Serenah." My hair pulled and my lips burned as he tried to gently rip the duct tape off me. As it came off my lips, he pulled me into his chest and held me there for a moment, comforting me, loving me. The warmth of his love rushed all over my body and began to ease my nerves down from the ledge they were standing on. Looking up at Charlie, I pushed my torn lips up to his and kissed him.

It was the sweetest kiss my lips had ever known.

He undid the duct tape that bound my wrists and then inspected the damage it left. They felt okay outside of a little soreness, but it wasn't okay to Charlie. Tears, but no words, poured out of Charlie as he brought the reddened wrists to his lips, letting his love fall onto them through his lips. He brought one of my hands to his cheek and looked me in the eyes and said, "It's over now, and you'll never have to worry again."

"I know," I said gently. "Thank you for everything, Charlie."

"I know it sounds weird, but I think I'm in love with you, Serenah."

"It doesn't sound weird at all. I love you too." It could have been the heightened emotions of hate, fear and uncertainty in the last few hours, but I felt it too. We both leaned in and kissed.

$\mathcal{W}$alking down the path through the flower beds to go meet with Emma about the *Inn at the Lake* on the dock, I admired the sunrise that was lifting into the sky. The painted beauty of God's design wrapped around me. I had called Emma last night and requested to meet with her at the dock in the morning. Seeing Emma sitting in a lawn chair down at the end of the dock with a chair next to her, I smiled.

As I walked the length of the dock, I saw a fish jump in the distance. The lake was peaceful and calm like it always was early in the day. As I came between the lawn chairs to sit down, Emma handed me a cup of coffee.

"Thank you," I said, taking the cup.

"You're welcome. So when do you want to start?" Emma looked over with raised eyebrows.

Smiling back at her, I titled my head, "You guessed I'd say yes?"

She nodded slowly and turned her eyes back to the water. "Of course. You love this lake as much as I do, and John is in jail. You start Monday. I've already worked out the details of you leaving Dixie's. Wendy will get over it, but Miley was a little broken up when she heard the news. You'll have a room that isn't sanctioned for guests located on the lower level." '

"Presumptuous of you to think I was on board," I said. "But I'm glad. I was dreading the talk with Wendy about leaving, and poor Miley. I'm going to miss her."

Emma took a sip of her coffee and stood up. "I want to show you something."

Intrigued, I said, "Okay." We walked up the path to the house and climbed the stairs to the balcony. Going in through the French doors, she led me upstairs to the Mountain Suite. She pointed to the bed, so I took a seat. Going over to a nightstand, she took a worn red journal off the top and sat down beside me. "There is a journal in every room for the guests to write whatever they wish. They aren't mentioned when we give the tours when the guests arrive, nor is it encouraged or mentioned during the duration of the guest's trip. It's just something that is entirely decided upon by the guest."

"Wow. Neat. Do you read them?" I asked.

She smiled warmly and nodded. "Of course I read them. That's the best part of this whole place." She opened the journal to a random page and began to read out loud. "A Spiritual and relaxing weekend that left me in awe of God's ability to heal and restore the soul . . ." Emma paused and placed a hand over the pages and looked over at me. "Every guest that comes here leaves with something more in their life, Serenah, whether it's a healing weekend getaway for a young, single woman or a restorative night for a couple. Each story is unique and full of wonder."

"Wow. Have you witnessed to anyone about Christ?"

"Oh, yes," Emma replied nodding. "More nights than I can count, I have prayed with a hurting soul in these hallowed walls." Her eyes glowed as she looked around the room. "This inn isn't just a place to stay when you're tired. It's a place where miracles can happen and God shows His strength and power. That lake out there has helped even you."

Thinking of the day after John blackened my eye when I had come down, I nodded. "It really has."

"God's creation has *that* power on us. We just have to allow Him to work." Closing the journal, she placed it on the nightstand next to the bed and looked at me. "You're going to love it here, Serenah. I know it'll be a blessing to you as it has been to our family for generations."

Smiling, I leaned in and hugged Emma. "Thank you for letting me become a part of this."

Charlie's voice rang through the inn downstairs, alerting both of us. I smiled at Emma and said, "We're going to go for a float on the raft."

"Run along," she replied with a smile.

Smiling, I leaned in and hugged her again. My heart swelled with love and warmth as I heard my love's voice call out again downstairs. Releasing her, I hurried out of the room and down the stairs to fall into Charlie's warm embrace.

"She already knew I was going to say 'yes,'" I said with a laugh in my voice as I told him the news. "She already made the call that I dreaded."

He grinned. "Nice! You were hating the idea of telling Wendy."

I pursed my lips together as I nodded and turned toward the oversized bay windows in the living room. "This is going to be the new view every single day for me."

"You know how people say things get old after you get used to them?" he asked.

Turning to him, I raised an eyebrow.

"It's not true. You never get tired of this view." He wrapped his arm around my waist. After a moment, he turned to me and said, "You ready for that ride in that raft? I'm dying to show you the bird nest I was telling you about."

"Yes," I replied with a warm smile. He took my hand and threaded his fingers between mine, and we headed down to the water.

To love and be loved—it was all I ever wanted. Nobody could ever convince me that John truly loved me. Though he had played the role exquisitely in the beginning of our relationship and into the first parts of our marriage, he was nothing more than a self-deluded con artist. Charlie, on the other hand, was my real love of a lifetime. I knew his heart was pure and of a good nature—for God had hold of it. When a man's heart belongs to the Lord, he's able to show a love that is divine.

The End.

BOOK PREVIEWS

A REASON TO LIVE PREVIEW

Chapter 1

POUNDING COMING FROM THE FRONT door of his house on the South Hill woke Jonathan Dunken from sleep at three o'clock in the morning. Then the doorbell chimed, pulling him further away from his slumber and fully awake. He had only been asleep for an hour, as he had been up late the night before sketching building concepts for a client. He was the co-founder and sole architect of his and his brother Tyler's company, *Willow Design*. A company the two of them started just a few years ago, after Marie passed and Jonathan needed more work to throw himself into.

Pushing his eyelids open, he sat up in his bed, smoothing a hand over his face. *Who on earth is that?* He wondered. The doorbell chimed again, and he begrudgingly emerged from his bed and left his bedroom.

He traveled out from his room, through the long hallway, and down the glass stairs. As he entered the foyer, more pounding on the door sounded, edging his already growing irritation. He was ready to rip into whoever was on the other side of that door. But when he finally opened it, his heart plunged and the wind fanning his anger fell quiet. It was his sister-in-law, Shawna Gillshock, a woman he hadn't seen since the funeral four years ago.

Shawna looked just like he remembered her—a mess, her brunette hair disheveled, eyeliner mingled with rainwater ran down each of her cheeks. She was wearing a stained pair of ragged sweats three times too big and a ragged oversized hooded sweatshirt. He immediately noticed the sight of fresh blood on a cut near her left eyebrow.

"I need your help, Jonathan. I didn't know where else to go." Her voice was strained, filled with desperation. She jerked her head toward the car in the driveway. Sheets of rain and wind whipped back and forth in the night's air, dancing across the headlights of the car. "My dad wouldn't let me come to his house. I need a place for me and my daughter, Rose, to stay tonight. My boyfriend beat me again, and I'm leaving him for good this time. You're the only person I know that he doesn't know. Please?"

Jonathan was moved with compassion, though a part of him wanted to say 'no' to her. Deep down, somewhere beneath the pain and grief that followed losing his wife, he heard a whisper and felt a nudge. *Let her stay.*

"Okay. You can stay." He helped her inside with her luggage and daughter. The luggage she had brought didn't consist of much. A backpack and one suitcase. Once the two of them had everything inside the house in the foyer, he led the way to the guest room on the main floor of the two-story house. The room was tucked away at the end of the hallway. Opening the door, he flipped on the light switch. Two lamps, one on each nightstand on either side of the bed, turned on. Each of the nightstands, along with the dresser and crown molding, was stark white. The walls were a warm brown, not dark, but not light either. On the far side of the bedroom, near the dresser, was another doorway leading into an en-suite bathroom.

"Thank you so much for this." Her words were filled with genuine gratitude as she set her backpack on the bed. She turned and glanced at the TV on top of the dresser.

"How long do you think you'll be here, Shawna?" Jonathan was gently reminding her it wasn't a long-term solution but more of a friendly gesture in a time of need.

"Just a few days. I'm going to call my dad again tomorrow and see if I can convince him to let us stay there with him and Betty until I can figure something out."

The mention of her parents jogged painful memories that Jonathan had tried to forget. His parents had died his senior year of high school, so he only really had Marie's parents in his life. "Okay, and if he doesn't budge?"

Shawna turned to face him. "I'll figure something out. Don't worry about me, just thanks again for tonight."

Her daughter became fussy a moment later, a whimper escaping. "What's wrong, Rose?"

She touched her tummy. "I'm hungry."

"How old is she?"

Smiling, Shawna turned to him. "She's two. Talking away already. Do you have anything she can eat?"

Scrambling through the fridge in his mind, he shrugged. "Does she like tuna?"

"Um, not really. Do you have hot dogs, macaroni, or something more kid-friendly like that?"

"No, but there are eggs in the fridge. Sorry. I wasn't really prepared for you." He tipped a smile, trying to loosen the awkwardness and embrace the disturbance of the entire situation.

She laughed lightly. "It's totally fine. Eggs work great. She loves scrambled eggs. Thank you again, Jonathan. It means the world that you took us in tonight."

"Don't mention it. Do you need help cooking, or can you manage it?"

"It's pretty basic. I think I got it handled. You look like you need some sleep, so go ahead."

"I do need sleep. Going back to bed now. 'Night."

Leaving Shawna and Rose in the guest room, he shut the door quietly and thought of his late wife, Marie, as he made his way back to his bedroom upstairs. Shawna was his only sister-in-law, and she had made frequent appearances in his and Marie's life, but that had been years ago. Even back in the day, Shawna was always in need. Her life reminded him of a slow-moving train wreck in progress. Though her life was a wreck, Marie was always ready and willing to love on her and care for her when she was in need of her big sister. That was Marie's nature with not only family, but anyone who was in need.

Did you enjoy this free sample? Find it on Amazon

LIVING ON A PRAYER PREVIEW

Chapter 1

April watched as her husband slipped out of bed and went over to the closet to get dressed for work. Justin Bybee was a good man and he loved her and the children. She knew that, but she couldn't help but long for the days gone by . . . when he'd kiss her for no other reason than to kiss her, when he'd write her poems and cook for her. All of those days were in the past, and April found herself growing in her discontentment as he pursued his dream career.

That morning, after his car left the driveway, she rose out of bed. She made the bed and then got ready for her part-time volunteer job at the Christian school, Alturas. Her life-long dream was to be a school teacher, and by taking the part-time volunteer position last year, she hoped it would put her in the forefront of the list when it came to hiring a teacher. Though it had been over a year already, a few of the teachers were leaving at the end of the current school year. Hope was on the horizon for April.

Venturing downstairs to the coffee pot in the kitchen, April poured herself a cup of coffee and peered out the window overlooking their backyard. The sun was just coming up over the neighboring houses. With March nearly over, the snow was almost gone, but the mornings still carried a cold, wintry bite to them. It warmed her heart to know that spring was on its way and change was in the air. Seeing the frosted swing-set in the yard, she was taken back to a memory of Justin putting it together for the kids. He used to have more time for the family, more time for life outside of work.

Before he became a district manager of seven locations for Joe's Pizza in the greater Spokane area, Justin was a restaurant manager. He worked long hours, leaving in the twilight of the morning, but he always made a point to get home by five in order to eat dinner with her and the children. As a district manager, which he had been for the last five years, she was lucky to see him by seven at night, let alone five.

"Mom?" The soft sound of her sweet daughter Abigail's voice was a welcome interruption.

April garnered a smile as she turned toward her. "Good morning, sunshine."

"Are you okay?"

Her daughter's concern pierced the depths of her heart. No, April didn't feel okay, but that wasn't a conversation she'd have with her six-year-old daughter. Bending at the knees, she met Abigail at eye level. She wanted more than anything to fill her child, all of her children, with love.

"Yes, Abby. I'm fine. Run along and get ready while I cook breakfast."

"Did Dad already leave?"

Another sting radiated through her motherly heart. "Yes. He was in a hurry, but he loves you. I promise."

"Okay." Sadness weighed in her tone as she turned and left the kitchen. It pained April to know how much her husband's choices not only impacted her, but more importantly, the hearts of their three children. She could manage herself enough, but their kids too? They needed their father desperately. Abigail, Nathan, and Kimberly didn't deserve an absent father who barely ever saw them unless it was Sunday morning on their way to church in the car. To April, they deserved the man she married, the one who cared deeply and loved even deeper than she thought was possible. Would she ever get that man back again? God only knew, and God was her only hope of it ever happening.

Walking over to her thirteen-year-old son's room adjacent to the kitchen, she knocked and entered the room. Flipping on the light switch, she woke Nathan and then went to the next room over and woke Kimberly, their sixteen-year-old daughter.

Returning to the kitchen, she retrieved the eggs and bacon from the fridge and started to prepare breakfast.

The smell of bacon soon filled the air in the kitchen and brought with it her thirteen-year-old out from his room. Nathan wouldn't miss breakfast for any reason in the world, though Kimberly would for an extra few minutes of sleep.

Setting the cooked food out on the kitchen island along with the plates and forks, she smoothed a hand over Abigail's blonde hair and then kissed the top of Nathan's head. She then went into Kimberly's room.

"Last time I'm asking, Kimberly. Wake up."

With the blanket still over her head, Kimberly pushed out a muffled but intelligible word. *"Okay . . ."*

"I want to see you."

Sitting up in the bed, Kimberly pushed the blanket off and looked at her mother.

"Happy?"

She smiled. "Yes."

Going through the kitchen as her two other kids dished up their plates, she went down the hallway to the laundry room. Unloading the dirty laundry hamper of its contents, she began to sort laundry and fill the washing machine.

As she closed the lid, her cell phone buzzed in her pocket.

Pulling it out, she saw a text alert from Capital One.

Capital One: Your recent transaction attempt at McDonald's was declined due to insufficient funds.

April's heart dipped.

Shaking her head, she was reminded in that moment of the growing debt problem she and Justin were in. Her heart grew heavy.

Eyes watering and in the quiet of her laundry room, she peered up at the white ceiling slats. "God? Why is he this way? Help me . . ."

Did you enjoy this sample? Find it on Amazon.com today!

FREE GIFT

Cole has fought hundreds of fires in his lifetime, but he had never tasted fear until he came to fighting a fire in his own home. *Amongst The Flames* is a Christian firefighter fiction that tackles real-life situations and problems that exist in Christian marriages today. It brings with it passion, love and spiritual depth that will leave you feeling inspired. This Inspirational Christian romance novel is one book that you'll want to read over and over again.

To Claim Visit:
offer.tkchapin.com

ALSO BY T.K. CHAPIN

A Reason To Love Series

A Reason To Live (Book 1)

A Reason To Believe (Book 2)

A Reason To Forgive (Book 3)

A Reason To Trust (Book 4)

Journey Of Love Series

Journey Of Grace (Book 1)

Journey Of Hope (Book 2)

Journey Of Faith (Book 3)

Protected By Love Series

Love's Return (Book 1)

Love's Promise (Book 2)

Love's Protection (Book 3)

Diamond Lake Series

One Thursday Morning (Book 1)

One Friday Afternoon (Book 2)

One Saturday Evening (Book 3)

One Sunday Drive (Book 4)

One Monday Prayer (Book 5)

One Tuesday Lunch (Book 6)

One Wednesday Dinner (Book 7)

Embers & Ashes Series

Amongst the Flames (Book 1)

Out of the Ashes (Book 2)

Up in Smoke (Book 3)

After the Fire (Book 4)

Love's Enduring Promise Series

The Perfect Cast (Book 1)

Finding Love (Book 2)

Claire's Hope (Book 3)

Dylan's Faith (Book 4)

Stand Alones

Love Interrupted

Love Again

A Chance at Love

The Broken Road

If Only

Because Of You

The Lies We Believe

In His Love

When It Rains

Gracefully Broken

Please join T.K. Chapin's Mailing List to be notified
of upcoming releases and promotions.

Join the List

ACKNOWLEDGMENTS

First and foremost, I want to thank God. God's salvation through the death, burial and resurrection of Jesus Christ gives us all the ability to have a personal relationship with the Creator of the Universe.

I also want to thank my wife. She's my muse and my inspiration. A wonderful wife, an amazing mother and the best person I have ever met. She's great and has always stood by me with every decision I have made along life's way.

I'd like to thank my editors and early readers for helping me along the way. I also want to thank all of my friends and extended family for the support. It's a true blessing to have every person I know in my life.

ABOUT THE AUTHOR

 **T.K. CHAPIN** writes Christian Romance books designed to inspire and tug on your heart strings. He believes that telling stories of faith, love and family help build the faith of Christians and help non-believers see how God can work in the life of believers. He gives all credit for his writing and storytelling ability to God. The majority of the novels take place in and around Spokane, Washington, his hometown. Chapin makes his home in Idaho and has the pleasure of raising his daughter and two sons with his beautiful wife Crystal.

facebook.com/officialtkchapin

twitter.com/tkchapin

instagram.com/tkchapin